MY GRANDMOTHER'S BRAID

Alina Bronsky

MY GRANDMOTHER'S BRAID

Translated from the German
by Tim Mohr

Europa
editions

Europa Editions
1 Penn Plaza, Suite 6282
New York, N.Y. 10019
www.europaeditions.com
info@europaeditions.com

Translation by Tim Mohr
Original title: *Der Zopf meiner Grossmutter*
Translation copyright © 2021 by Europa Editions

Library of Congress Cataloging in Publication Data is available
ISBN 978-1-60945-645-0

Bronsky, Alina
My Grandmother's Braid

Book design by Emanuele Ragnisco
www.mekkanografici.com

Cover illustration © Ginevra Rapisardi

Prepress by Grafica Punto Print – Rome

Printed in the USA

MY GRANDMOTHER'S BRAID

I can remember the exact moment Grandfather fell in love. In my eyes, he was ancient—already over fifty—and his new, delicate secret hit me with a wave of admiration tempered by schadenfreude. Up to then I'd always thought that I was my grandparents' only problem.

I sensed that Grandmother wasn't supposed to know about it. She'd already threatened to kill him for far lesser offenses, like when he crumbled bread during dinner.

I was nearly six and knew a thing or two about love. While in preschool in Russia I'd fallen in love with three caretakers in a row, sometimes the affairs even overlapped. In the nine-story apartment block where we'd lived before we emigrated, there wasn't a girl under eighteen that I hadn't at least had a brief crush on. When my grandmother noticed my gaze lingering on bouncy skirts or ponytails on the street she held her hands in front of my eyes. "Careful your eyeballs don't pop out of your head. You'll never get a girl anyway."

In silent protest against this prophecy, I subsequently fell in love with a woman I'd never seen. I saw her name on a poster and just liked the look of it: Rosa Silberstein. At home I hummed the five syllables of her name to myself over and over again until my grandmother listened more closely and ordered me to cut out the nonsense, things were grim enough as they were.

Not long afterwards we arrived in Germany as quota refugees and Grandfather met his love.

At the refugee home, we were, as Grandmother noted unhappily, surrounded by Jews. She'd never made a secret of her antisemitism: "Not because of Jesus or anything. I have genuine, personal reasons." She'd nearly burst whenever she had to keep herself from using certain curses during toasts with the neighbors. Then she'd revel in the fact that she'd managed to gain access for us to the privileges of the golden West under false pretenses. "Just so you don't think we're really Jews," she hammered home to me while feeling my forehead for a fever, "Opa had an uncle who had a brother-in-law. He had a Jewish wife. That's why we're here. That's how it works. Don't ask."

I nodded eagerly, as if I'd been convinced of something as a result, or at least understood. I'd never seen an uncle of my grandfather, not to mention the wife of his brother-in-law. Generally I tried to avoid talking to Grandmother unnecessarily, first and foremost because I never knew what sore spots my questions might expose. I barely remembered crossing the border, except for the fact that Grandmother immediately seemed disappointed.

The home was a former hotel with a cracking plaster façade and a sign still adorning the entrance that said "Sunshine Inn." Most of the residents walked to synagogue on Friday evenings, where, after services, there was a buffet that was both lavish and free of charge. Grandmother ironed my blue pants every Friday and cut my fingernails so she didn't have to be ashamed of me. She was intimidated by the real Jewish children.

Despite her distaste, she would never consider skipping Shabbat. She grudgingly honored it by dressing up: she coiled her dyed red braid atop her head like a snake, and made her polka-dotted dress festive with the addition of a silk flower at the neck. Behind her show of confidence I sensed her deep fear of being exposed as an imposter and being sent back to the collapsing Soviet Union.

While the shabbiness of the refugee home disappointed

Grandmother, the shiny, new synagogue elicited a respectful word or two. She wholeheartedly welcomed the fact that women sat separately from men during services: "I'm happy not to have to see their grouchy mugs for a while." She sought out the neighbors she knew from the refugee home and ensnared them in long conversations at the cold buffet before she inconspicuously—she thought—swiped this or that food item.

The next morning she'd unwrap the rolled pancake or savory pastry from the napkin and dish it up for Grandfather. I was permitted only to watch: the food had been touched by strangers' paws and was therefore not fit for me to eat. As she was serving breakfast, she went over all the previous day's conversations. Grandmother looked unfavorably on most of the new acquaintances: she was suspicious of people who left their homelands, except when it came to us.

"Of course, there are also some decent people," she said on one single occasion, and Grandfather and I listened closely. "I met a delightful woman. Her name is Nina and she teaches piano. Lives here with her daughter. The girl's Maxi's age, but normal. No husband, lucky her, bringing up her illegitimate daughter all alone. You know her, Tschingis, you carried a sack of potatoes upstairs for her once. Why would she need so many potatoes when it's just the two of them? You'd let me break my back but you'll play the gentleman for others."

My grandfather's hand twitched for a second, and the filling of ground meat and leeks burst out of the pastry he was eating.

QUACK

In Germany, Grandmother took me to the pediatrician. Actually, she explained to me on the way, this was the real reason for our emigration: to finally be able to take me to an upstanding doctor for treatment, one who could give hope to me—and more importantly, to her—that I might survive into adulthood, even if it meant Grandmother would have a millstone around her neck for decades.

She had my medical files with her, they were bound in leather and looked like the rediscovered handwritten manuscript of a lost classic. The files were filled with diagnoses, glued-in blood and urine analyses, and unreadable notes from various specialists Grandmother had consulted and who had regaled her with conflicting opinions. Slips of paper or prescriptions sometimes slipped out of the files, and Grandmother quickly gathered them up and stuffed them back inside.

The German doctor's office was colorful and bright, and the memory of the Soviet polyclinic, with its painted-over windows and hygiene warnings full of threats and commands, seemed like a fever dream. A mountain of toys rose on the worn carpet. I knew that I wasn't allowed to touch any of them. Anything that Grandmother hadn't personally disinfected was contaminated with germs. Still, I enjoyed just looking at them. The nurse weighed and measured me and gave me a smile that made the back of my neck warm.

To Grandmother's indignation, we had to go back to the

waiting room after that. It was full of children of different ages, all of whom were spreading diseases. One coughed, others sneezed, and Grandmother suspected the ones without obvious illnesses were hiding contagious rashes beneath their clothes. She pulled me frantically onto her lap, and I was definitely too old for that. Though she had publicly humiliated me so often that I felt immune to nearly any embarrassment.

"If I'd known about this chaotic situation, I'd have brought facemasks," Grandmother said, trying to wrap her scarf around my mouth and nose, which suffocated me and itched horribly. "Now sit still, Grandma's not a trampoline."

"I'm suffocating," I rasped.

"Asthma?!" She rummaged through her bag for the spray—she'd brought a large number of them across the border with us out of precaution—without bothering to free me from the stranglehold of the scarf.

Luckily we were called into the examination room at that moment. The doctor was a man, which my grandmother approved of enthusiastically, since she trusted men more, at least when it came to medical questions. She smacked my medical files down on the table. "Chronic bronchitis, chronic sinusitis, chronic gastritis, moderate myopia, vegetative-vascular dystonia, allergies, diminished growth, mumbles, decelerated reflexes, decelerated cognitive development, early childhood trauma. But you can see for yourself." She spoke only Russian.

The doctor bent forward with a furrowed brow. With one hand he shielded himself from my grandmother's stream of words while he stretched the other out to me. After a moment's thought I took his hand. From the German words directed at me I was able to filter out some I knew, laid myself down on the examination table, and pulled off my T-shirt.

The doctor sat down next to me and listened to me with the stethoscope, holding up his hand every time Grandmother opened her mouth. He shined a light in my ears, pressed around on my throat, and knocked on my back. This last thing I took as an encouraging sign.

"What?" said my grandmother when he made a waving gesture in our direction. "What does that mean—*Tschüß*? What does *gesund* mean?"

I explained it to her when we were out on the street and she had stuffed the medical files back in her bag.

"How do you know that?" she asked. "Who taught you? We only just arrived, and you're an idiot."

I shrugged. In my fist I held the gummi bear I was allowed to take from the jar as we left.

"What a quack," said my grandmother. "He didn't take any X-rays. Even our drunken hags are preferable to that. What do you have in your hand? Can't you see the bacteria stuck to that thing? Do you want to get sick? Give it to me."

I handed her the gummi bear and Grandmother popped it into her mouth.

BIRTHDAY

The nurse's smile had made me remember why life is beautiful despite it all: there are women everywhere. The first weeks in Germany had gone by in a fog, and now I felt as if I was waking up again.

I'd always thought of women whenever I felt a cold claw gripping my heart. Grandmother had started to prepare me for my demise very early. The notion that time was trickling away gave me a sensation like goose bumps, and I wanted to soak up as much beauty as possible. I loved everything about women. The thin ones were lithe and fragile like daddy longlegs. The sturdier ones radiated warmth and plushness. If women were big I admired their strength, and if they were small I regretted the fact that I couldn't protect them. That my grandmother was also a woman never crossed my mind.

On every birthday Grandmother greeted me with the words, "Oh miracle, thanks be to heaven and myself, he pulled it off again." She gave me socks and mittens she'd knitted herself, and later presented me with a giant cake, the sight of which always plunged me into despair. I knew how it would end even before Grandmother announced: "Look, once again Grandma spared no cost or effort and hunched over my work all night. Chocolate cream, three layers. The freshest eggs available here. Take a good look at it, from every angle. What do you think? It tastes divine, you must believe me."

I believed her immediately without even asking whether I could try a slice. I knew the answer so well that I could recite it to myself: "Do you no longer need your pancreas? This kind of food is for normal people. You can eat it with your eyes, which is healthier anyway. You may also smell it." She dragged her finger along the cake plate and held a creamy dollop up to my nose.

I'd never had any friends, which I thought was normal, because my grandparents didn't have any, either. In Russia, Grandmother had usually invited one or two random neighbors for my birthday, but they never came back again. My seventh birthday came around during the first months in the refugee home. I wondered whom Grandmother would invite this time so as not to have to eat the cake alone with Grandfather.

Grandmother found the Germans suspicious from the start, and besides, she didn't know any—setting aside the unsatisfactory exchanges of words with the pediatrician or the refugee home's maintenance man. "We have to stick to the Jews," she concluded with resignation, inviting the delightful neighbor with whom she'd chatted about my streptococcus at the synagogue. "Nina's her name. Can you remember that? N-I-N-A. Very polite, fine fingers, not surprising given her profession. Don't scare her off, you philistine idiots."

It was my grandfather who opened the door for Nina and stepped silently to the side to let her into our little apartment, which consisted of two hotel rooms that had been combined since our little family represented a "married couple with male child." For a brief second he flinched and it seemed as if he wanted to keep her from entering the barely existent foyer and his life. Then he took the crucial step to the side. She came in and grazed him with her shoulder as she went past.

Nina looked as if she'd been drawn with a soft pencil. She had a pretty parcel with her, which Grandmother took from her and quickly stowed in one of the cabinets. A girl entered the room behind the visitor, and she looked like a little copy of her mother.

"Delightful girl," said Grandmother before the guests even had a chance to say happy birthday to me. She poked me in the back so I'd make space. "Please sit right down! The tea will get cold. Tschingis!" She shoved my motionless grandfather to the side. "What are you standing around for, go get another chair. Nina's daughter, you can sit here on the couch. Careful with the tea. Scalding is the worst kind of injury you can get. I only ever give my idiot the cup once it's cooled." She put a half-filled cup of tea on the windowsill for me.

They were our first guests on German soil. Since the kitchen was too small, Grandmother had set the table in the larger of the two other rooms. The table was pushed next to the couch where she and I slept at night. "Now please sit down, dear Nina. Tschingis, aren't you listening? You're sitting here."

We sat around the table and Grandmother talked. When the conversation turned to me, which was often the case, I felt a look of concern from Nina and one of schadenfreude from her daughter.

"I don't know how I can send him to school, dear Nina. Here they want six-year-olds in the first grade, the cruel bastards. How can one possibly let a creature like this out of the house? That would be irresponsible of me. He can barely digest anything, and the other pupils will make mincemeat of him, don't you think?"

"I would hope not," said Nina kindly. I didn't dare look in Grandfather's direction.

"You're a teacher, you must have experience with children who are mentally and physically disadvantaged." Grandmother kept her focus on the visitor.

"Unfortunately not," said Nina. I felt a twinge: I would have liked it if she'd contradicted Grandmother, which some people actually dared to do when they first met our family, they expressed their astonishment at the assessment of my mental and physical condition. The bravest among them even suggested that there was nothing peculiar about me at all, which was brushed aside by Grandmother with an, "As if you know anything!"

"What are you sitting around for, Tschingis? I baked, with my own hands. With the best ingredients. No garbage from a confectionary shop. I don't want to poison anybody."

I followed with wistful glances as the big slices of cake were put on plates and slowly disappeared. In front of me was placed a plate with a greenish mound on it that slowly turned brown. My tea was still cooling on the windowsill.

"Pay no attention to him, dear Nina and Nina's daughter. I grated an apple for the poor lump, unfortunately it's all he can digest. My work never lets up."

Grandfather sat there silently. I wondered if it was the first time I'd ever seen him focus so intensively on someone, or if I just never noticed because Grandmother's presence completely dominated my attention. Because it seemed indiscreet to continue to try to read Grandfather's feelings, I turned my attention to the girl, who had a nice, round face but who started to kick me under the table.

"You're a happy woman, Nina, because you're single and have a normal child. Just look how delightful she is. So quiet and polite," said Grandmother while I tried to maneuver my shin out of kicking range.

"Your son makes a nice impression, as well," said Nina.

"My son? You're just flattering me. I don't have a son, never had one. I'm an old woman long past menopause. This creature is my grandson. What all I've endured with him. Every year counts double for me."

Nina remained silent, shocked.

"But that guy," said Grandmother, gesturing toward Grandfather, "he still looks like a boy even as an old bag. It's the Asian genes. They just don't age. Their skin is much thicker than us whites', understand? They just keel over at some stage. Heart. Tschingis, say something."

Grandfather sat upright. Grandmother's stream of words just beaded on him and rolled off like a summer rain.

"And how Jewish are you, Nina? A quarter? An eighth? You just look too delightful."

Nina took a sip of tea. Something in her face changed. I cringed because it looked at first as if she were about to break out in tears. She held her cup in front of her mouth for a long time, and I slowly realized she was trying to stifle a fit of laughter.

"One hundred percent," she said, setting the cup down silently. She smiled at my grandfather and I watched with fascination and horror as deep red crept up his dark cheeks. I'd never seen him blush before, and I crossed my fingers beneath the table in the hope that my grandmother wouldn't notice it.

"We'll see if you manage another year," said Grandmother as we lay next to each other on the sofa that evening and she tucked the covers all around my frail body so as not to give the drafts any chance, even though it was thirty degrees in the shade. My birthday celebration had put her in a sentimental mood, and I worried she would hug me now, or worse still kiss me. In an effort to divert Grandmother from threatening me with tenderness, I fell back on a reliable game: "And what if I don't? Will I have a nice funeral?"

My calculation was correct: Grandmother's eyes began to shine. "The nicest," she assured me fervently.

"Like the one for dear Maya?"

"At the very least."

I was satisfied. Maya was the good child Grandmother had raised before me. In Grandmother's memory Maya was an eternal girl, bigger than me at the end, but never grown up. Her stories about Maya were short and confused. Sometimes I begrudged Maya her angelic existence, after all I'd been a curse in human form since my first breath, and direct comparisons weren't any fun.

"And when I'm buried, you and Opa will come?"

"Who else, dummy."

"And maybe also Nina and Vera?"

"If they have any decency."

"And who else?"

"Don't be troublesome. Maybe the red-haired Jew."

The red-haired Jew was a frightening figure from Grandmother's bedtime stories. I didn't think it was fair of her to include him now. The nice atmosphere evaporated. I rolled onto my side.

"You know what?" said Grandmother. "You need to learn piano."

"Why?" I sat back up and the carefully tucked covers fell from around me.

Grandmother had always dissuaded me from learning anything up to now because it would have been too taxing for me. That's why I'd kept it from her that I could now read passably and do a bit of math, because I'd kept cautiously asking Grandfather about various letters and numbers. For two years now I'd been able to tell when Grandmother got fleeced at the market. When she accused merchants of cheating her, it was without fail the wrong ones.

Grandmother yawned loudly. "You could give recitals. Earn money, buy Grandmother a house. Nice white one, garden in front, like the Germans. My brother learned how to play the piano. His teacher used to smack his knuckles with a ruler and cried a lot."

"Why?"

"Why what?"

"Why did *she* cry?"

"It's obvious. Because he couldn't play, dummy. She told our parents they should rather have him learn boxing."

I said nothing.

"They didn't let me try an instrument at all at first," mumbled Grandmother drowsily. "Because apparently I broke everything. What nonsense. But I always listened at the door and learned more that way than my brother, rest his soul. You know what, actually you don't need piano lessons. What good would it do? Who would you play for? And when? You don't have too much time left anyway."

"But the German doctor didn't find anything serious."

"I'll tell you something, Maxi: that is the worst sign."

Among Germans

On my first day of school, Grandmother got up at six. She went about what she referred to as "prettying oneself up," which she normally did only for the weekly visit to the synagogue: she plucked her eyebrows and put on blue-green eyeshadow. She woke me up and called me down to breakfast in a hoarse voice.

"Why so early?" I whined, the covers wrapped around me.

"So you have time to digest in peace," she said. "You can't go to the bathroom at school, the toilets are full of germs."

"But I don't need to go right now."

"Of course you do. It's just a question of discipline."

I spooned up what was on this day particularly watery oatmeal. It felt as if it would stick to my intestines. I used the moment when Grandmother left the kitchen to empty the contents of the bowl into the sink and wash it down the drain with plenty of water.

I sat back down just in time, as Grandmother came back and cast a glance at the sink. "Did you throw up?"

I nodded. I faintly hoped she'd let me stay home, but she just patted me on the head. "It's the anxiety. School is hell."

Grandmother threw a couple pens and notebooks in her large cloth bag, combed my hair with a side part, made sure I had a long-sleeved undershirt beneath my sweater, and led me by the hand out of the apartment. We crossed the hallway and beneath a pale, threadbare carpet, the wood floor creaked in sympathy. We stopped in front of Nina's door. Nina's daughter, Vera, was in the same class as me even though she was ten months younger. As Grandmother was knocking, signaling it was time to walk together to school, I tousled my hair, ready to blame it on a draft.

Nina opened the door in a robe. She looked alarmed.

"Is something wrong? It's only seven."

"Maybe for you. But for me it's nearly noon. I have to speak to the teachers." Grandmother rolled her eyes dismissively and took my hand. So began my school career.

"You can't be here during class." The young teacher looked the way I sometimes pictured my mother: blonde, slightly wavy hair, blue-green eyes, and a few freckles on the bridge of her nose. As a matter of principle, Grandmother never spoke about my parents. "Don't speak of the devil," she yelled if I tried to ask about them.

"He won't get along on his own." My grandmother poked me in the back so hard I nearly stumbled into the teacher. "Translate it for her!"

I passed along her words. The teacher's eyes widened. "That's extremely unusual," she said.

"What does she want, Maxi?"

I told Grandmother in Russian. She grabbed my ear, pulled me upwards, and with the other hand made a sweeping gesture from high to low, indicating my whole personage.

"Look at him. Does he look as if he can be on his own?"

I translated.

"Honestly, yes." The teacher smiled encouragingly at me. I'd never had so many women smile in my direction in my entire life as I had in these early days in Germany. "He even understands the language."

I translated.

"He doesn't understand anything. Where is he supposed to

have learned? From TV? He's an idiot, he can't add two and two, and he knows half the alphabet at best."

I translated.

"That's why children go to school. To learn to read and write."

I translated, full of wonder at the beautiful woman's calm.

"Other children will beat him up."

"Please don't worry."

"Never been alone without supervision."

"We have twenty-four children in the class, and do you see any other parents here?"

"He's a poor orphan."

I stopped translating, I couldn't keep up anyway. I felt bad for the princess-like teacher. I knew what she didn't yet know: that she didn't have even the slightest chance against my grandmother. Though she held out longer than I would have expected.

Grandmother pulled out my medical files. She'd invested a small fortune in the translation and notarization of every scrawled note about my health after she'd been unable to find a German doctor who would confirm the diagnoses. Grandmother kept complaining to Grandfather that the local doctors obviously weren't as well trained as those in the Soviet Union, as they hadn't even heard of some of the conditions. Grandfather patted her hand.

"Please convey your concerns to the school administrators." The teacher suddenly seemed worn out. She was no longer smiling and wasn't looking in my direction anymore, either.

Grandmother nodded and left, only to return some time later. She smiled triumphantly and took a seat at the back of the room with feigned nonchalance.

The longer Grandmother held out in the back row, the more hardened she became in her belief that the education system was "like in Africa"—her most disparaging description of a broken state of affairs. It irritated her that students were permitted to go to the bathroom anytime and that the teacher allowed us to eat and drink during class without first checking our hands for germs or the lunchboxes for banned foods.

The work we were assigned wasn't making Grandmother any smarter, either. But this didn't stop her from hurrying to my place as soon as anything was passed out, putting on her glasses, and explaining particular terms to me, though she was nearly always wrong. Even in everyday life, only with much luck could she effectively use her handful of German words, and in school she had utterly no chance. The small chair disappeared beneath her when she joined group exercises and dictated nonsensical answers to me. In order to keep her busy, I dreamed up little problems for her and I let her color in the pictures on the math worksheets.

She followed me step for step during recess, too, and prevented every attempt I made to mingle with the other children. While I stood at the edge of the schoolyard and watched my fellow students at frenzied play, she bent toward me and wiped my mouth or forehead with her handkerchief and whispered:

"Don't ever play with the little Turk, he has crazy eyes, like he's about to bite. And do you see that girl? Her posture is nearly as bad as yours, she'll be wearing a corset for scoliosis in a few years, mark my words. Hey, watch out with that ball, you Aryan freak, or else I'll have a kick-around with your head! You see how lively normal children are? Why are you standing around next to your Oma like a sack of flour?"

But little by little the homework got too complex for her and standing around the schoolyard too boring. Grandmother began to bring her knitting for her hours in the back row. One morning she snapped at me that she wasn't a watchdog and couldn't guard me around the clock. If Germany insisted I was of school age, then Germany would have to make sure I stayed alive at school. She pressed into my hand a list of foods that would surely kill me, made me promise to tape the list to the classroom door, and said her goodbye at the front gate of the school.

"And don't speak to the red-haired Jew!" she called after me as I ran across the schoolyard, barely able to believe my luck.

"What?" I stopped abruptly and went back to her. I had long since come to regard the red-haired Jew as a character out of fairy tales, like Baba Yaga or the seven dwarves. "Is he real?"

"What do you think? That's why you should never tell strangers your name. Got it?"

"Even at school?"

"Why not at school?" Grandmother exploded. "They're already watching you. Just imagine that you're out in the schoolyard and a stranger comes to the fence and calls you. You should definitely not answer, understood?"

"Does he really have red hair?" I asked, bewildered.

"How should I know?" Grandmother waved me aside and turned to go. As she did, she bumped into Vera, who was trying to maneuver past her with her jacket open and a bubblegum bubble in front of her mouth.

"Dear child!" Grandmother changed her tone immediately. "Always on time. Will you keep an eye out for Maxi when I'm not around? I'll pay you a mark per week."

Vera cast a mocking look at me and sucked the bubble back into her mouth. For a moment I was worried the gum would get stuck in her windpipe. "Two marks."

Grandmother leaned her head pensively. "She's smart, too."

Grandmother never tired of warning me about my classmates. She impressed upon me that I was not only physically weak and mentally deficient but also that I had a cursed appearance that made people want to beat me up.

When I brought my first class photo home, she circled the

children who'd seemed suspicious to her during the weeks she spent sitting in my classroom. She analyzed their facial expressions, sorted them by last name and origins, and made a ranking of the most dangerous classmates.

"The Turks are feral," she enlightened me at the kitchen table, though she didn't distinguish between Syrians, Afghanis, and actual Turks. "If they see you and your idiotic grin, it's lights out. And you can't appeal to their parents, they live in clans, and complaining doesn't do any good. Have you heard how the Golden Horde captured Kiev in the old days? But of course you don't have history lessons, you just draw things with crayons. Just don't tell anyone that you have anything to do with Jews. They'll scalp you straight away."

I shuddered. I had slowly come to doubt the truth of some of her assertions, but when it came to sowing fear, Grandmother was still very convincing.

"Chinese," she said, circling with her pen the face of a classmate whose mother was Vietnamese. "Stick close to her, but don't trust her. She doesn't want you to be better than her, and she'll lie to you."

"I don't even talk to her."

"That's a mistake. You should talk to her, learn her tricks. But then again who wants to talk to you. Stay close to the girls, they probably won't knock you around as badly, but don't play with them or else the Turks will take you for gay. Understand?"

Yes," I croaked.

"Do you feel coldy? Open your mouth. Stick out your tongue out and say *Ah*. Sure enough, throat's red, full of streptococcus. There's something on your tongue, could be fungal, that'll eat you from inside. You listen to your Oma."

Her prophecies didn't come to pass. Nobody tried to beat me up. Ever since the time of Grandmother's accompaniment at school, I'd been considered untouchable, and my classmates' gazes went right through me as if I were invisible to them as well. They tripped over my feet once in a while and then ran off without even turning around. Nobody wanted to know what percent Jewish I was. There was only one child who overtly hated me and who also always had to sit next to me because the teacher, despite our protests, thought we were best suited to work on group projects together "as a result of our similar backgrounds."

Whenever Grandmother found bruises or scrapes on me during her regular checks, I made up a different Arab name to confirm her suspicions about a violent gang that was always after me. I would never in my life disclose that the injuries were inflicted by a girl being paid to watch out for me: Nina's daughter, Vera.

Grandfather stood at the window, motionless. It had gotten dark and I could only make out his silhouette. Every once in a while I wondered whether he was even still breathing. At some point Grandmother noticed, too. She put down her glossy magazine and went over to him inquisitively.

I knew what there was to see. Nina came home around this time. She usually crossed the courtyard with a bag of groceries followed by Vera, who dragged her schoolbag behind her. They both disappeared into a rear entryway, and a few moments later the light went on in the second-floor window across the way before the curtains were drawn and then only shadows were visible behind them. When Nina was late, Grandfather waited until she finally arrived. Sometimes she reemerged shortly afterwards with a bag of garbage: an unexpected gift that conjured up a faint smile on Grandfather's face.

It was strange to me that my grandparents were now standing there together. Suddenly Grandmother became animated, waving and knocking on the glass.

"Look! It's Nina! Where'd she get that jacket?"

Grandfather took a step back and looked away.

"She's moving out the week after next," said Grandmother, still pressed to the window.

Grandfather's back slumped. I spoke for him: "Really? Why?"

"Everyone leaves. Normal people have proper apartments thrown their way. She was in a particular hurry to get out of here, I heard. Found a place with two rooms, a kitchen, and a bathroom. I think it's because she plays piano. We're the only ones who have to waste away in this dump because your Opa would prefer to look out the window than do something for the family."

"She won't be there anymore," I said.

Grandmother poked Grandfather in the back. "Won't you even lift a finger? Single woman with dependent, helpless in the world. We're upstanding people, you have to help her."

Grandfather said nothing.

"Without a man, lucky her," said Grandmother pensively, and not for the first time, when discussing Nina's situation. "But somebody has to hammer the nails into the wall. She has those delicate musician's fingers, can't do anything else in life. That's what happens. Tschingis, help the poor woman move."

Grandfather nodded without making eye contact with her. I heard an accelerating hammering and slowly realized that it was his heart, which in some mysterious way seemed connected to my own, making his excitement pump through my body as well.

Grandmother shook her head. "Gather up the junk you brought from home. Screwdrivers and whatever else. So slow on the uptake, this man. Have to spell everything out."

Only later did it become clear to me that Grandmother hadn't come up with this initiative out of pure charity alone. She'd been trying for quite some time to deepen her relationship with Nina. "A respectable woman," she told me. "Pleasure to know her. You don't have to worry about suddenly having a knife in your back with her. A rare thing these days. Ninety-eight percent of immigrants are untrustworthy." She'd already knocked at Nina's door a few times in vain, as Nina was either not there or hadn't opened the door.

While other children in the home were scared of my grandmother, Nina's daughter Vera regularly sat at our kitchen table. Grandmother had sweets and presents at the ready in order to lure Vera to our place after school, almost like the child molesters she warned me about in her bedtime stories. As far as I was concerned, the fact that she paid Vera to look out for me at school was enough, especially since Vera wasn't exactly dutiful about that. As soon as she had dragged me across the schoolyard and shoved me into my seat she didn't look out for me at all—aside from the occasional kick under the table. Though she had no difficulty giving detailed reports about my school days if Grandmother asked.

"He didn't do much. Actually he didn't even move."

"That's how he is, dear Vera. He's got no strength. Did anyone mistreat him?"

"No. They all know I'm looking out for him." Vera didn't even blush saying that.

"But even you can't always have your eyes on him." Grandmother sighed.

While Vera unwrapped a new doll, Grandmother laid our homework notebooks side by side. She compared the work, complaining the whole time about my scrawled handwriting. "Look how neatly a girl writes. If I could I'd make you into a girl, Maxi, but it's too late for that, unfortunately. Don't listen to old Margo, Vera, she just admires your handwriting. Every single letter is perfect, no wonder you get good grades. You'll finish school with honors, go to college, have a career, and marry rich. And you, shrunken-head? Nothing to say? Vera, dear, when's your mother coming home? I need to talk to her."

At some point Grandmother finally managed to catch Nina in the courtyard. She asked her straightaway about my musical education. Nina took a step back, Grandmother took one step forward. She held Nina's sleeve, just to be safe.

"It's well-known that it's never too early to expose children to the wonders of music, dearest Nina."

"But you say yourself that the boy is already overwhelmed with the material in first grade."

"The teacher teaches pure nonsense, the child is dumber than when he started school. Music could be helpful for Maxi's development."

"To be honest, I don't trust myself to teach such a special student."

"There's nothing special about him, he's just falling apart."

"Exactly, I'm just not attuned to that." Nina made every effort not to look at me.

"Think it over, Nina. I ask no more than that. I know that even Jews have a heart, and you are such a delightful person. My husband will help you with your move. We have no ulterior motives behind that. Let your conscience decide."

I hadn't really believed that Nina would soon be moving out. I was used to things being promised without ever being fulfilled. In Russia, Grandmother had always talked about how we needed a larger apartment, but we'd never moved. I was still waiting for a promised trip to the seaside, as well as the annually promised Christmas tree. The promise to move to Germany was the only one that had ever come to fruition—and that one, out of all of them, Grandmother had kept a secret because she feared we'd be stopped at the border. So even as we packed we never mentioned the name of the country where we were going lest the nosy neighbors who were no doubt listening through the walls would cause problems.

Nina taught me that some promises came to pass more quickly than I could grasp their momentousness. The move that came so suddenly to me kept not only her but also Grandfather busy. He helped her pack her things into the two suitcases they'd come to Germany with and whatever was left into a few moving boxes. He carried everything down to the little panel van that he'd personally arranged to get. Afterwards he spent what felt like weeks at Nina's new apartment. There were walls to paint, used furniture to assemble, a stove and washing machine to set up, grouting in the bathroom that needed to be redone. Grandfather came home late on those days and usually went straight to bed. Sometimes he'd get up in the middle of the night and slip out. When I went to the window I'd see him smoking next to the trash bins in the courtyard.

"Look at that, the old man's become a tradesman," said Grandmother when Grandfather, just home from Nina's, disappeared into the shower. "That woman has him slaving away. And here at home nothing gets done anymore. Must I mop the floor myself so you don't suffocate from dust?"

I nodded, because that seemed the safest option.

"Now you nod, too? Are you on his side? Have you two made a pact against me? Do you want to slip something into my food?" She brooded for a moment and suddenly changed her tone. "Wouldn't it be nice to learn to play music, Maxi? Sit there so spiffy at the piano in a tuxedo? Show me your fingers. Might as well get rid of them, you won't go far with those short sausage fingers. But at least you can't hurt yourself doing it."

It was my grandfather who took me to my first piano lesson at Nina's new apartment. It seemed only fair to me—without him, Nina would probably never have agreed to teach me. I was worried that Grandmother would be jealous of this new arrangement, was sure of it, in fact, getting to sit behind me during the piano lesson like during the first weeks of school. But she brushed it aside: "I have enough to do. Opa can also take care of you—don't lose the child along the way, you hangman."

Grandfather took my hand. His hands were raw and dry like paper. His grip was strong and gentle at the same time, and I enjoyed not having anyone pull me along or complain that I was going too slowly or too fast or had sweaty palms, which could be evidence of a fever or lung nodules or even my impending demise.

From the first step outside our building I felt like I was on a world tour. Up to then my life in Germany had rarely extended beyond a small radius that included my home, my school, and the pediatrician's office. Anything beyond that made Grandmother nervous. Her discomfort spread to me, so that I always felt relieved to have survived any longer trip—to a Russian-speaking dentist, for instance—without any long-term damage.

The silence emanating from my grandfather gave me the chance to observe the surroundings and discover amazing things: the fluttering leaves at the top of the trees changed colors with the direction of the wind, switching between light green and silver; ants ran busily along cracks in the asphalt; and nobody, and I mean nobody, paid any attention to me.

I hopped onto the streetcar with Grandfather and my brief happiness was replaced with sudden panic.

"Here!" I said and pulled him to the front seat, directly behind the driver. According to Grandmother it was the safest seat in a streetcar. She'd taught me since I was little to always sit behind the driver in buses and cars, as well. "If something happens, he'll instinctively steer in a way that keeps him from harm. And you're directly behind him—even better positioned!"

If the seat was taken, she shooed the unlucky occupant away: "Make room for a little invalid. Some people!" If there weren't two seats then Grandmother remained standing, since she already had her life behind her. She shielded me from other passengers with her body and shot angry glances around.

Grandfather apparently wasn't aware of this seating system, but gave in at my insistence. There was only one seat free behind the driver, and to my horror, Grandfather sat down in it. I wasn't prepared for this eventuality, and I didn't know what to do. Just standing there seemed an impossibility. Grandmother would never have allowed me to remain standing during a ride since I might be flung against people, windows, or doors. But making my way through the carriage to look for another seat, on the other hand, would mean losing contact with my minder, which was no less risky. I clutched the support pole.

Grandfather didn't notice my distress. He patted me on the head lightly. It seemed as if he wanted to say something. But he remained silent. His glance alighted only briefly on me, then shifted out the window. Grandmother would never have let me out of her sight in a situation like this, she always locked her sky-blue eyes on me as if it took all the power her soul could muster to hold onto me, to protect me, and to get me through life.

Slowly I calmed down because nothing happened and I had survived standing through two stops already. I watched my grandfather. Furrows ran across his broad forehead like plant rows through a freshly plowed field. His skin was much darker than my grandmother's, darker even than my own. His eyes seemed to have no pupils. When she was in a good mood Grandmother called Grandfather Steppenwolf and Nomad Child, and in her extremely rare moments of happiness she talked about my grandfather's family, who went around with yurts and sheep and put buffalo milk in their tea.

I'd tried many times to picture it, but never managed. My grandfather drank his tea with sugar. Grandmother's stories came across like fairy tales.

When I was still little, I'd assumed Grandmother had kidnapped Grandfather so that he'd help her with everyday tasks and run little errands for her: go shopping (even though he brought home the wrong stuff every time), repair a table, stand on a chair to change a lightbulb or grab canning jars off the top shelf.

Grandmother had a fear of heights. Once she stood up on a low stool and broke out in tears because she was so panic-stricken that she couldn't get back down. Grandfather hurried over to her and held out his hand, led her to a comfy chair, and held her hand until she calmed down. At that moment I realized he was with her voluntarily and that, unlike me, he could leave anytime.

Nina opened the door right after the first ring, as if she'd been waiting for us. She stood there in jeans and a men's shirt that caressed her soft outline, looking past me to lock eyes with Grandfather. At first I thought she was upset with him because she didn't say a word, not even hello. Grandfather also remained silent, but that was normal to me.

I stood between the two of them and stared at the shiny buttons on Nina's shirt. Grandmother would never have dressed like that. She always changed clothes as soon as she got home because everything she'd worn on the street would spread germs inside the apartment, not to mention that they'd get additional unnecessary wear and tear. Unless she was hurrying to synagogue, when she went out she wore one of her two floral cotton dresses or her new tracksuit, within the walls of the apartment she wore an older tracksuit the color of which was difficult to identify anymore. If the tracksuit was in the wash, she put on her bathrobe. I preferred the bathrobe because I had the impression that it put Grandmother in a milder mood and pleasantly slowed down her motions.

Nina smiled at me. "Hallo," I said, electrified and helpless like a hair that's been rubbed against a balloon. "I'm not allowed to stand in the draft because of strep."

Nina apologized and let us come inside. She called my grandfather by his first name and asked him to wait in the kitchen. From the depths of the apartment a sleepy Vera emerged.

"Put on the teakettle," said Nina drowsily to her daughter.

I watched as she walked away and marveled at the courage she had to face the dangerous act of making tea. I was always shunted out of the kitchen as soon as anything was on the stove. When I'd once asked Grandmother about the point of this safety measure, she'd shown me pictures of children with burn wounds that gave me nightmares for months. I wondered if I shouldn't fall in love with Vera. But for ages I'd only been able to get excited about women and girls who were taller and older than me.

"And you're interested in music?" asked Nina as we sat side by side at her piano.

I shook my head. Her eyes were the color of German milk chocolate, and for this reason alone I never wanted to lie to her.

"Grandmother says music is nice," I mumbled.

"Does she like music?"

"I think so."

"Does she listen to a lot of music?"

"No. She listens to the radio sometimes, but only for short periods of time because she says she can't concentrate on it anyway because of the voices in her head." I paused, fascinated by the two creases that suddenly appeared on Nina's otherwise smooth brow. "The voices know everything," I quickly explained so she didn't get the wrong idea. "They tell her what's going to happen, they can predict the weather, and they know which people lie."

Nina put her hand on the music rest and remained that way for a while, her face turned away from me. "Would you like a cookie?" she asked.

"I'm not allowed," I said.

"Oh, O.K." She stood up and left the room.

I pushed on one of the keys. They were astonishingly loud, I let my finger walk along them, skipping some, then playing only the white ones, and finally only the black ones. The piano was old, the yellowed keys reminded me of my grandmother's teeth. She was proud of her well-preserved set of teeth, though most of all about her gold tooth, about which she said: "When I'm dead, don't forget, it's your inheritance. You can buy yourself a house with it if we don't have one by then."

In the next room Nina was talking to Grandfather. The walls were thicker than at home, and I couldn't make out their words. Still, I was fascinated by the deep male voice coming from the kitchen, a voice that was foreign to me, as if it was somebody I didn't know doing the talking. Nina's voice, on the other hand, sounded high-pitched, she seemed overexcited and perhaps even upset, which didn't fit with my image of her.

I wondered how my grandfather could have managed to exasperate her so much. His voice was still even keeled and reminded me of a jeep driving slowly but steadily along a bumpy back road. I tried to find the key that made the most similar tone and found it pretty far toward the left end of the keyboard. I played it over and over again. Then I found another key to play Nina's role and let the two notes talk to each other. At some point my grandfather fell silent; more time passed, which didn't bother me because I enjoyed every moment alone. Nina returned and there were red splotches on her face. She sat down next to me on the piano bench and shook her head.

"Awful," she said. "What do you think of me now?"

I didn't think anything of her other than that she looked good in her checkered men's shirt.

"If you were a hummingbird—which key would you flutter on?"

I understood that she took me for an idiot, just like my grandmother did, but I still performed the exercise to her satisfaction along with the next one: where did I think an elephant would be?

"And here," I said, "is Tschingis."

I proudly showed her the key I had discovered. When she didn't answer, I looked over at her and was startled: she had tears in her eyes. I thought frantically about what I could say to comfort her. Luckily I remembered that nothing makes women as happy as compliments about their children. So I leaned toward Nina and assured her that Vera looked very healthy today.

On the way home I was permitted to sit next to Grandfather and drum my fingers against the window. I imagined that I was playing on an invisible piano keyboard, until Grandfather covered my hand with his large palm and pulled it away from the window.

"Which notes did you learn?" asked Grandmother after Grandfather delivered me home and she'd patted me down to make sure I'd survived the outing intact. Grandfather retired immediately upon returning home to the cot in the adjoining room.

"The old man's all tired out, eh?" said Grandmother. "Thought kids just raised themselves." She combed my hair with her fingers and called me her future pianist. It was unusual to experience Grandmother being so satisfied with me, and I suspected that it wouldn't last long.

I pointed out to her that nobody could learn an instrument without practicing regularly. This surprised Grandmother, but in the end she agreed. Since we didn't have the space or the money for a piano, she had Grandfather look into getting a small and inexpensive alternative. Two days later he came home with a plastic keyboard.

The new toy had red and white keys and several buttons that triggered tinny melodies. When I discovered how to do this, Grandmother, hearing multiple notes in succession, came running from the kitchen, where she'd been cleaning the meat off a beef bone that had been boiled for hours. She was disappointed that the keyboard was so far ahead of me, called me a talentless idiot, and went back into the kitchen.

I was afraid that Grandmother would accompany me to my weekly piano lesson from now on, in order to discuss my lack of progress with Nina. But surprisingly she seemed resigned to the idea that the task belonged to Grandfather, who, every Thursday, put on his shoes a few minutes early and waited for me to gather up the sheet music and disinfectant wipes. I enjoyed the silent rides on the tram, the three-quarters of an hour at Nina's and a few quiet minutes sitting on the bench at the tram stop while Grandfather smoked a cigarette at a safe distance.

At home Grandmother tried to quiz me, pointing to individual notes in my book and asking me to name them. Just for fun I purposely mixed them up. She never noticed.

This made me bolder. When she asked me about my math homework I claimed that in Germany there was an entirely different multiplication table. I satisfied Grandmother's interest in Nina's moral conduct by suggesting she had a man—an idea I was proud of because I had the impression it got Grandfather out of the line of fire. I claimed never to have seen the supposed lover, but to have seen things in Nina's apartment that hinted at his presence: giant slippers in the hall, an overflowing ashtray on the kitchen table, even a screwdriver on top of the dresser.

My fabrications were helped by using props I actually did notice at Nina's apartment and about which none of the adults ever said a word. There really was a new pair of slippers at Nina's, for my grandfather, though his feet weren't as giant as the ones I dreamed up. Grandfather smoked, though unlike the lover in my version, he only smoked out on the balcony. There was a cup out there that served as an ashtray. And he tinkered around with something in Nina's apartment during every piano lesson, as if he wanted to justify his presence, but he never left tools sitting around. He wasn't as sloppy as the made-up man, who in my mind was so unlikeable that I didn't think he deserved Nina. When I had the feeling that Grandfather with a facial expression or Nina with an indiscreet word was letting something slip, I would like to have covered my eyes and ears. Sometimes it was as if a delicate plant was growing in Nina's apartment, one that was threatened by strange looks but that I could protect with words.

"Is he German?" asked Grandmother after she'd listened to my tales with her nose turned up. "Probably. They're upstanding, like your grandfather."

"No idea," I said.

"I'll tell you something, Maxi: these things don't last for long."

We were in the second grade when Vera stopped pinching me and kicking me under the table. I had put up with her wrath without fighting back because for one thing it didn't hurt as much as she probably wished it did, and for another it fascinated me that Vera could look so much like her mother and at the same time be so different.

Nina was the gentlest person I'd ever come across. I felt all the tension inside me melt away as soon as I entered her apartment. I assumed it was the same for Grandfather. Since I couldn't practice much at home, Nina kept me busy with scales or sang the Internationale with me, a song that Grandmother also treasured, and which, when she was in a good mood, she demanded I play a plastic version of on my keyboard, the sound of which I could barely stand.

As soon as I was able to play the first few easy melodies, Grandmother remarked on my abilities. She wanted more hits from her youth: "Millionen blutroter Rosen" and "Bella Ciao," which she was convinced the Italians had stolen from the Soviets, just like the Americans stole the Russian classic the *Wizard of the Emerald City*. Nina shook her head when I insisted on these songs, but she made easy arrangements for me and asked me with a smile not to tell anyone I was taking lessons from her.

I relished every second in her apartment, as if with the step across her threshold I was released from gravity, weightless. I could make mistakes, ask stupid questions, look out the window. I could go to the bathroom and not prove afterwards that I'd washed my hands twice. Sometimes I hugged Nina, and I never figured out whether it was related to the piano lessons or her temperament, maybe both. I begrudged Vera her mother, but would never have admitted it because it would have seemed like a betrayal of my pretty blonde freckled mother whom I'd never seen because Grandmother didn't believe in photos.

It gradually began to make me sad that in front of me, Grandfather and Nina still acted as if they had nothing to say to each other, as if the third toothbrush in the bathroom really did belong to the faceless man I'd made up, as if the familiar cigarette pack next to the tea cannister in Nina's kitchen had been forgotten by a visitor. The more Nina's apartment felt like my grandfather's second home, the more my thoughts revolved dizzyingly around the fact that there was more than one version of every life.

Maybe it was possible, in theory, for me to do something other than slurp pureed cauliflower while watching Grandmother redo her braid.

The piano lessons felt like a short trip to a world I wasn't allowed to live in. After the lesson Nina sent me to the kitchen where there were cookies and tea on the table. Grandfather smoked on the balcony and she went out and stood with him for a while every time. From behind the fluttering curtain the contours of their shoulders seemed to blend together, one entity with two heads with smoke hovering above. Normally I enjoyed the fifteen minutes alone, dunking cookies in black tea and then letting them dissolve on my tongue. But suddenly I couldn't sit still anymore. I grabbed a cookie and went down the hall, standing in front of Vera's half-open door.

Vera was lying on her stomach reading a comic. She sat up immediately and stared at me with her big, light-brown eyes.

"You play wrong notes all the time."

"I know." I went into her room and sat on the edge of the bed, amazed that she didn't immediately shrink away from me.

"She cries every night," said Vera, and she didn't sound as indignant as usual, she sounded quiet and unsure. "Does he do the same thing?"

"He's a man," I said. "He's just silent."

"Why on earth are they doing this?"

I shrugged my shoulders.

"I'm going to tell your grandmother."

I choked on the cookie in horror.

"You can't do that," I coughed as Vera struck me between the shoulder blades. "You can never do that. She'd kill him. And Nina. And me. And maybe even you!"

"Nonsense."

"Yes she would. She already tried to poison him once."

Vera stared at me with her mouth open: "With what?"

"Rat poison," I said. "But she grabbed the cup from him and poured it down the drain."

"But why?"

"Because she still needs him."

"No, I mean why did she want to poison him?"

"I don't remember," I said. There'd been so many incidents that had gotten jumbled together in my head.

Vera made a face. I saw her foot move in my direction like in the good old days, but then she held back. I rubbed my shin anyway, which throbbed with phantom pain.

HALF-AND-HALF

Grandmother often chided Grandfather about us being poor.

"What is the point of dragging the child to the West if we can't feed him properly and are dependent on German charity?" she ranted as if it had been my grandfather's idea to emigrate. I'd never understood what profession he'd practiced before, Grandmother mostly referred to his occupation as "not worth talking about." At the home he'd begun to fix leaky faucets and heaters because the building's maintenance man preferred to tinker on his own car than on the building. Soon Grandmother printed fifty sheets of paper saying "All Jobs Done Cheap" with our phone number and stuck them up on lampposts.

Now Grandfather spent much less time on the cot in the adjoining room. There were days when he left the apartment at dawn, while I sat at the table and choked down chicken broth, and only came back when I was already half asleep on the pull-out couch and Grandmother was oiling her heels with goose fat. He pushed carefully through the narrow gap between the door and the bed, whispered hello, and disappeared into the adjoining room, as my grandmother said in a low voice: "Where were you all day? I spend twenty-four hours a day dancing around the sick child and he gallivants around, and the piddling amount of money he brings in just makes you want to cry."

Grandfather said nothing. I lay next to Grandmother and pretended to be asleep.

The next morning, after being yanked from sleep by the alarm, I saw Grandmother sitting at the table counting money. She smoothed the bills and stacked them neatly. She never seemed to be happy with the height of the stack. She shook her head and clicked her tongue scornfully. "It's as if he's paying for the privilege of painting a fence," she mumbled as soon as she noticed I was awake. "Any normal man would have made at least twice as much."

I lay in bed and marveled at how close to the truth she had come. I was sure that Grandfather was giving exactly half of his earnings to Nina, once he'd taken out a small sum to cover his cigarettes and newspapers. Like Grandmother, who was sure Nina was being supported by someone, I didn't believe that Nina earned enough to live off by teaching piano, either. Once Nina stood up in the middle of a lesson, as if she couldn't wait a second longer, and went into the adjoining room. Through the open door I saw her throw bills in Grandfather's face.

"As if I need your charity! Shall I also cut half of you off, an arm, a leg?"

Grandfather got on his knees, collected the twenties, and pressed them into her hand. He held her right hand tightly in his two hands. That day I plonked away on the same few chords of my children's version of "Schwarzen Augen" all alone. Nina never returned to the piano. My grandfather's shirt had wet spots on the shoulder which dried in the wind on the way home.

My warning not to tell Grandmother about Nina and Grandfather seemed to have made an impression on Vera. She spoke more to me now, which wasn't always a good thing.

She asked questions. Lots of questions. In her style of talking things out, which felt like a punch to the gut, Vera resembled Grandmother. She asked me why, even now, Grandmother watched over me when I went to the playground. Why she

carried my schoolbag and why she brought a thermos of medic-
inal herb brew to the school door, why she fell to the ground in
front of everyone on the street one time with a scream so loud
it rattled the neighborhood just because I was holding a soda
can in my hand that actually belonged to her, Vera, and from
which I'd only taken a sip to see whether my stomach would
really disintegrate. (It didn't, but I had also spat out the soda
straight away.) Whether my grandmother was really the witch
she was seen as, whether she was totally off in her head or only
a bit, why I washed my hands before *and* after eating, whether
I really was allergic to animal and human hair, whether my
mother had possibly sold me to my grandmother or if perhaps
I'd been kidnapped. Vera's tactlessness fascinated me, and I put
genuine effort into satisfying her curiosity.

Grandmother continued to regard the foreign children with
a mix of fascination, envy, and suspicion. The blond German
children steadfastly refused to understand her, which even led
to her saying one time that there were apparently children who
were more idiotic than me. They spurned the waffle candies,
the shortbread with nuts and condensed milk filling, and other
goodies from the nearby Russian supermarket that Grandmother bought in moments of nostalgia, the wrappers of which
she let me smell. Vera, on the other hand, not only accepted
the sweets, she also now sat willingly at our kitchen table, supposedly to help me with my homework. Unlike my grandmother I knew what was on her mind: if Grandfather came
home and glimpsed Vera, she enjoyed the brief pained spasm
of bad conscience that animated his otherwise expressionless
face.

"Explain it to the idiot, dear child, explain it to him,"
Grandmother said, hovering over us as Vera and I bent over
our notebooks and nudged each other with our feet. The kicks
of her earlier phase had given way to tentative and sometimes
almost caressing movements that tickled like crazy.

"I used to be so good at math, but German math is different somehow, and he doesn't believe his grandmother knows how to do it properly. He takes his grandmother for stupid, that's how it goes for the elderly. At some point I'll no longer be needed at all, and then he can dance on my grave. Doesn't matter, I'm still going to leave him my gold tooth. Would you like to see it, too, dear child?"

"You're not old at all," Vera responded and took a bite of the sweet Grandmother had pressed into her hand.

"I am old, dear girl, every year counts double for me. If you look at it that way I'm over a hundred. And in that case I still look good for my age, eh?" As Vera continued to chew, I got an affectionate smack on the back of the head from Grandmother.

"Your mother must be thankful to have such a clever daughter, independent and healthy, spit three times over your shoulder, break a leg. How's Nina? Is she healthy? She's single, the lucky woman, though sometimes one can feel abandoned in a strange land."

Vera mumbled something and clamped her teeth onto the chewed end of her pencil.

"Take that thing out of your mouth, dear child, you'll get splinters, they'll puncture your esophagus, it's an excruciating way to die."

Vera ignored the advice. Instead of explaining the homework to me, as Grandmother asked, she had long since put my notebook next to hers and copied my answers. Then she sharpened her pencil with my sharpener and didn't empty it. The ticking of the clock grew louder when Vera disappeared into the bathroom forever and didn't wash her hands afterwards and I asked myself why Grandmother didn't notice despite the fact that she lectured total strangers about the dangers of cholera and dysentery. I would have loved to watch that argument with Vera, but the hours went by and always ended the same way: when Grandfather opened the door in the evening, she was always sitting there and smiled at him.

"Here comes the old man, hungry as always, spent more money than he earned, wash your hands. No, don't sit down at the table, you're old and can wait. This girl here needs to get home first, there's a lot of Turks on her street and you can see the Jew in her, I don't mean that as an insult, dear child, surely you've looked at yourself in the mirror. Accompany her to her door, we're not animals, after all. Shall I make you a sandwich for the road?"

Grandfather demurred with a turn of the chin. He looked at Vera and in his gaze was a plea for forgiveness that I didn't like: he was my grandfather after all, not hers.

I didn't begrudge Grandfather his increasing absence and rarely thought about whether he really needed to stay elsewhere for nights on end for work and how much of that time was being funneled to Nina. I was less generous when I realized he was being guided by some strange sense of fairness with regard to Vera. When he came home from a few days away he brought me little gifts—one of the few expenditures he allowed himself beyond his cigarettes. At least I thought so, until I noticed too many similar things in Vera's room for it to be a coincidence.

If my grandfather gave me bubbles, there would be an identical bottle on Vera's desk. If he brought me a teddy bear, its twin jumped into view on Vera's bed. The fact that he drew so little distinction between a strange girl and his grandson confirmed what my grandmother always claimed: nobody in the whole world would ever care as much about me as she did.

"And perhaps the red-haired Jew," she added reliably.

"There's no such thing," I tried to object sometimes.

"Don't believe your Oma, huh," scoffed Grandmother. "But what do you say to this: when you were five months old, he stole you from your stroller. Fact. I parked you in front of the bakery, the stoop was too high and not a soul would help me. And he went straight for you and grabbed you. I ran after him, yelled for the militia, and ripped you away from him."

"And what happened to him?" My grandmother's power of persuasion was enormous: I really had the feeling that a blurry memory would suddenly emerge in my mind's eye, a contorted face with a twitchy eye, the relentless pulling on my limbs from the opposite direction.

"Ran off, the coward," Grandmother said with disdain.

"But what did he want?"

"Nothing good, that's for sure."

"But did he want me? Maybe he didn't have any children of his own?"

Grandmother snorted. "What's with all the questions? Don't believe your Oma? Maybe one day you will grow up after all. And then you'll stop orbiting me. Leave me to croak without so much as a glass of water. Just forget me. Humans are ungrateful animals."

It seemed impossible that I could ever forget Grandmother. She took away the teddy bear that I got from Grandfather because she said it stank of chemicals and she gave it to one of the snot-nosed neighbor children. A comic book I got from Grandfather ended up in the garbage because it was trash that would destroy my brain. I mourned it and finished reading it in Vera's room. I also found out that my grandfather had taken her and Nina out for ice cream. On the way home from piano lessons I demanded Grandfather apply his fairness principle consistently. I wanted ice cream, too.

Grandfather looked at me. I withered beneath his abysmal gaze. I felt a bit ashamed for my demand and was surprised when Grandfather slowly nodded.

My hand in his, we entered the ice cream shop. It wasn't that I'd never been in one before. Grandmother loved ice cream. When she bought ice cream and I was with her, she sometimes let me hold the waffle cone while she disinfected her hands with wet wipes. But now, when the person behind the counter asked me personally what kind I would like, my head was abuzz. Overwhelmed from the offerings I pointed to a container filled with a pink mass while Grandfather ordered peppermint. We took our cones out into the fresh air and sat on a bench.

Only when Grandfather had finished his ice cream did he notice that I'd not even tried mine. "Doesn't it taste good?" he asked, stretching out his hand to dip his finger in a pink drip. I shook my head. The ice cream was melting in my hands, and I felt as if I were holding a live grenade with the pin pulled.

Sometimes on nights when I couldn't fall asleep because my stomach was rumbling with frustration at rice gruel and oatmeal, I would imagine what all I'd devour if I had only a week left to live. With the end in sight, I thought about chocolate cake with frosting, pancakes oozing with Nutella, the fried dough balls filled with jam that I'd seen once in a while in the window at bakeries. I tossed and turned with those images in my head until Grandmother got up, groaning, and went to find a sedative in her bottomless medicine bag. I remembered nothing about the following two days.

The viscous pink mass dripped down my fingers. My grandfather figured out what was going on in my mind and reached out his hand to release me from my agony. But I held on tight to the sticky cone. He went back inside the ice cream shop to get a few napkins, and in this moment I decided it was worth it: I would lick my fingers and then fall over dead.

When Grandfather returned with a stack of napkins I was just busying myself chewing up the last of the cone. When melted there was ridiculously little ice cream. He correctly interpreted the look on my face and got me a second cone.

When I was dead and gone he could finally move in forever with Nina and buy Vera comics and bubblegum, I thought, as

I bit into the second ice cream cone, which hurt my teeth. Then I waited for something to happen to me.

We walked to the tram station. Along the way, Grandfather stopped to moisten the paper napkins at a fountain and helped me wipe off my hands and mouth. It was as if we were getting rid of the evidence of a crime, and I thought for a second about the aggressive German fountain water germs and the fact that they'd immediately colonize my guts and lungs and cause me a torturous death.

My stomach cramped up, but the pain didn't come from what I had eaten but from my panicked, slumped posture and frantic breathing. Grandfather lit a cigarette even though I was right next to him.

It was naïve to believe that a crime like that could escape notice by my grandmother. When we entered the apartment, she was sitting cheerfully at the kitchen table knitting wool socks for me. Grandfather tried to slip past her into the adjoining room. Grandmother took a loud breath. Her nostrils quivered.

"Did you smoke in front of the child? Have you completely lost your mind?"

"It was at the tram stop," I blurted desperately. "There was a strange man there! He was the one who smoked a cigarette!"

"What was the point of having your grandfather with you? Couldn't he grab the cigarette out of the pig's mouth and shove up his backside?"

Excited at the choice of words, I forgot my fear for a moment.

"Opa is too old to fight," I said quietly.

"Too old? This stallion? Have you seen how he carries boards and pipes around? Asians don't get old. I'm the only one getting old here."

I put out my hand and patted my grandmother on the arm. For a moment her face softened, but then her eyebrows came together menacingly. She grabbed my hand, turned it over, sniffed it. My heart stood still.

She shoved me away with surprising force—I fell backwards and hit my head against the wall. She ran into the adjoining room, where Grandfather was just putting his shirt over the back of the chair. Like a crazed pit bull Grandmother fell upon him, ripping at his undershirt, pounding him with her fists.

"All sense pounded out of you or what?" she screamed while my grandfather tried to shield his face with his hands. "What did you give the child? Why not just give him rat poison? Do you care about the child at all? Killed Maya and now get rid of the kid as quickly as possible? Not with me around. I'll put you behind bars."

I leaned my throbbing head against the wall and closed my eyes. Grandfather didn't answer. My grandmother's punches became less frequent and hollower. Suddenly it got very quiet. I looked cautiously into the adjoining room.

Grandmother had her eyes closed and was leaning against Grandfather. He was holding her in his arms, his cheek nestled against her temple. His shoulders and upper arms were scratched, as if he'd run through a blackberry bramble.

They stood there for what seemed like an eternity. I held my breath, unable to move.

TWO CRIMINALS

The strawberry ice cream that I'd unexpectedly survived taught me two things: Grandmother was wrong more often than I'd suspected, and happiness was easier to find than I'd thought. The colorful world of forbidden foods suddenly opened up to me. Of course, for ages I'd looked at all the sweets on the supermarket shelves, in the window at the bakeries and the downtown food stalls, but only now did I realize all I needed to do was to reach out my hand. I told Grandmother that from now on I needed pocket money. She looked at me over the rim of her glasses: "What for? Naked girls?"

"What naked girls?" I asked, confused.

"In the papers."

"Which papers?"

"At the newsstand!" Grandmother roared. "How can anyone be so stupid? Ask your grandfather."

I didn't think for a second about doing that. And I didn't get any pocket money. "Money doesn't come for free," Grandmother said. "If you don't work, you don't eat."

"But you don't work."

Grandmother calmly put down her knitting, picked up a teacup, and threw it against the wall. It was the wall I was standing against, and I assumed she hadn't meant to hit me. But one of the shards did hit me and I yelled, "Ow!" loudly even though it hadn't hurt. I wanted her to regret her outburst. But anytime I intentionally tried to stoke fears about my physical well-being, it never worked.

Grandmother stood up with a sad look on her face and retrieved a brush, which she pressed into my hand.

"So I don't work? And who caters to you day and night?"

I began to sweep up the shards.

"Give it me, said Grandmother without moving. "You'll cut yourself, the wound will get infected, your finger will have to come off, and what use will you be then?"

"Nobody needs me anyway," I mumbled, on my knees to appease her.

"True," said Grandmother.

For a moment I wondered whether she would pay me to work. I could take on some of the daily chores and receive an allowance in exchange. But as hard as I thought, I couldn't come up with any suitable tasks. My grandmother, as I realized through this exercise, didn't do much around the house. It was mostly Grandfather who mopped the floors and cleaned the bathroom. She really just looked after me, and I could hardly relieve her of that.

That's how I became a thief. I helped myself to her purse from time to time. I pulled out her wallet, took a few coins and one of the small bills, and quickly put it back. The first time I was worried she'd notice. But she didn't seem to keep close track of the contents of her wallet. That also explained all the useless bits of paper that made it difficult to find money at all, the telephone numbers of Russian doctors written on receipts and ripped scraps of newspaper, tattered pickup slips for laundry or repaired shoes, never-used prescriptions for glasses.

With the stolen money in hand, I was a free man, and bliss could be bought. During the lunch break, unlike my fellow students I didn't go into the shop across from school that sold soap and insecticide where you could also pick out gummi worms from a big plastic bin. I went directly to the discount shop around the corner where I bought a large chocolate bar or a packet of chocolate-covered marshmallows. I sat back on a park bench and ate everything up in minutes, until my gums stuck together and I had a sugar rush. Afterwards I slunk back to school, thoroughly washed my hands, and rinsed out my mouth. I felt better than ever during the next few classes.

My happy buzz dissipated when Vera caught me on the park bench with one of my treasures. I tried to wipe my chocolate-smeared mouth clean, as it was too full to get out an excuse. Vera was still getting money from Grandmother to spy on me. I held out half of the chocolate bar to her silently. She sat down next to me, broke off a small piece, let it dissolve on her tongue, and then stuck the rest in the pocket of her jacket.

"You're disgusting," she said. But she didn't tell on me.

Not long afterwards Grandfather caught me with Grandmother's wallet in my hands. The frantic way I tried to stuff the wallet back in the purse was more embarrassing to me than the fact that I'd been exposed as a thief. Grandfather shook his head. Then he put his hand in his pocket, pulled out a tenner, and handed it to me. I took it with trembling fingers and put it in the waist of my pants. I tried not to look him in the eyes. We were both criminals and covered for each other.

DANCING GIRL

Over time I realized that Grandmother felt lonely. Grandfather was gone more and more often, almost every day and sometimes at night, and he didn't draw a distinction between workdays and the weekend. I had no idea whether he was distributing advertising circulars or selling drugs. Even if I'd turned into Vera for a moment and asked him directly—I couldn't imagine getting a straight answer out of him.

My mornings at school were straightforward, but sometimes I made up additional activities, claiming for instance that I attended a special class for foreign students where homework was done under pedagogical supervision. There was nothing like that at our school, but Grandmother believed me straight away and even somewhat begrudgingly praised the German school system for the first time. In reality I did my homework during breaks while sitting on a heater.

That's also where I spent afternoons reading all the books I could take out of the school library and was reluctant to bring home because Grandmother would always insist I translate the first few sentences for her to make sure the book had literary merit.

Since Grandmother now had plenty of time, the laborious overcooking and pureeing of vegetables gained the upper hand. She prepared cauliflower and broccoli in a steamer and crushed the vegetables with a fork, as if I had no teeth. Sometimes she was already cooking before I got up and filling plastic containers with unsalted vegetables and buckwheat to give me for my ever longer school days. Sandwiches were only for alcoholic bachelors, neglected latchkey kids, and Germans.

Since I flushed the contents of the containers down the toilet and stuffed myself with sweets instead, I gradually grew not only taller but also wider. At some stage Grandmother stopped calling me Sack of Bones.

"Finally he's beginning to digest," she said to my grandfather, pinching my fat rolls.

It didn't help much to combat the loneliness. In her desperation, Grandmother began to address strangers on the street. She sat down in her tracksuit next to young mothers at the playground and told them they should put hats on their children. She looked into strollers and made faces that made the babies start to cry. Grandmother caught in midair pacifiers that had been spit out, but refused to give them back because they were no longer sterile. The mothers switched benches and after a while they left the playground, while my grandmother called valuable advice after them in Russian. She knocked on the neighbors' door to ask them about the weather in Moscow, but they didn't have the faintest interest in the topic.

"Typical Jews," Grandmother commented with frustration. "Sold their home for a better life. But if things go poorly for them in Germany, I'll tell you something, Maxi: they'll turn their back on the place without a thought, the disloyal people."

I was choking down a helping of celery that Grandmother had served me as a snack between lunch and dinner. She'd sat down across from me, her chin resting on her folded hands, greeting every gulp of mine with a nod of her head. She asked me whether I'd understood anything in school today. The devil must've gotten into me when I pulled a vegetable fiber out of my mouth, put it down on the edge of my plate, and said: "Nina is directing the choir club now."

I hadn't even finished the sentence before it was clear to me what a mistake it was. Grandmother's eyes lit up.

"What does that mean?" she asked.

"No idea," I sputtered unconvincingly.

"Idiot," said Grandmother. "I'll call Vera."

"It's a sort of school club, in the afternoon, where every-body sings," I said eventually.

Grandmother was silent, and, full of misgivings about what the future might hold, I ate every last bite of the vegetables and slipped away.

Later that night in bed I heard Grandmother lay everything that had been fermenting inside her for the past few hours at Grandfather's feet. "I'm not so old that I'm no longer useful. I've molded that little cripple from a maggot into a calf, he hasn't failed a grade yet even in Germany, and who deserves the credit for that? I was a good dancer, and have talent as a teacher. I'm going to make sure that these fat German girls no longer lumber around like sailors, I can teach them a thing or two. I can, can't I, Tschingis?"

Her voice sounded pleading, and she said my grandfather's name almost tenderly. On the way to the bathroom I cast a glance into the adjoining room to assure myself that nobody had switched my grandmother with a stranger.

"Get in bed, you tadpole," she yelled as soon as I stuck my nose into the doorway. Relieved, I went back to bed.

The fact that Grandmother had once been a dancer I'd always taken for a joke. Though she sometimes pointed to the television screen when a famous politician or actor popped up and claimed to have once met the person. She'd crossed paths with Muhammad Ali when during a visit to the Soviet Union he'd slipped his many guides and minders and was strolling all alone down the street, and she also met this singer who looked a bit like a woman and who had asked her for directions and she fixed his tie, which was all askew. Later I found out that this must have been David Bowie. In any event I usually just looked at my feet whenever Grandmother talked about her stage career, and she smacked me on the back of the head. "Don't believe your Oma, eh? Do you think the old lady was always unhappy and ugly?"

I did indeed think that, until one day Grandmother pulled a suitcase out from under Grandfather's cot, a suitcase that had been there since our arrival as if to be ready at any moment to pack up and move on. I wasn't allowed to touch it, and sometimes I wondered if perhaps my mother's bones were stored inside. Now Grandmother opened it, shoved aside some moth-eaten things, pulled open the zipper of an inner pouch, and pulled out an envelope. A half dozen photos and several tattered newspaper clippings fanned out before my eyes.

"What do you say now, doubting Thomas?"

I picked up a picture and held it in front of my nose.

"Nearsighted!" bellowed Grandmother. "Look, Opa, he's blind, and we didn't notice."

I quickly moved the photo farther from my face. In it were four girls who were a few years older than me. They held each other by the waists and looked at the camera. They were standing on their tiptoes, and their feet were in what to me were magical ballet slippers, and the starched skirts offered a view of four sets of slim girls' legs on which the muscles stood out.

"Did you recognize me straight away?" asked Grandmother.

I nodded even though I spotted no resemblance in any of the girls. One had a pouty mouth, another looked sad, the third smiled, and the fourth was laughing as if somebody had tickled her. I studied the three thoroughly before coming to the fourth. She had high cheekbones and the perfect lines of her neck and waist left my throat dry.

Astonished, I looked at my grandmother then again at the girl. If this is real, then anything is possible, I thought. In that case then Boris Yeltsin really did have her over for coffee. And perhaps other things were true, too, that I had taken for, if not bold-faced lies, then at least distortions.

"Can I have this photo?" I asked hoarsely.

Grandmother nodded, flattered.

I put the photo down in front of me and tried to draw the face of the girl. I didn't know myself why it was so important to me. Of late I'd only used my colored pencils to add horns and stuck-out tongues to the faces in the photos of the Russian newspaper Grandmother took from the supermarket. Now it seemed to matter that I transfer the face from the snapshot as exactly as possible onto paper, as if I could deliver the girl from a destiny she didn't foresee at the time of the photo.

Out of the corner of my eye I noticed Grandmother throw first the jacket and then the pants of her tracksuit onto the chair and squeeze herself into something that looked like a bathing suit that she'd dug out of a nondescript bag inside the suitcase. I'd only rarely seen her without long sleeves on, and I'd never paid any attention to her legs. I'd have suspected that beneath the tracksuit her body was soft and flabby. But in reality she looked like one of those heavy athletes I'd seen during sports broadcasts on television. Beneath the creased skin moved muscles, and I realized, shocked, that Grandmother was also a strong person physically. If she decided to, she could easily break my slim grandfather's neck, not to mention mine or delicate Nina's.

She spun around, straightened her back, lifted her arm. I had my head leaned down over the paper, now I lowered my gaze to her feet and gulped. Grandmother was standing on her big toe.

"You're staring, eh?" she said with satisfaction. "What are you drawing? Show me. Is it a rabbit?" I looked at her face and could have nearly screamed: suddenly I couldn't deny recognizing in her face the traits of the girl in the photo, as if my grandmother had devoured her alive, as if she were still sitting somewhere inside her body, begging to be let out.

Grandmother hadn't let me in on her plans. So I was horribly startled when I ran into her in front of the school office.

I didn't recognize her right away. Instead of the tracksuit she was wearing a long sequined dress that brightly reflected the sunlight. She had festive blue-green eyeshadow around her eyes. Her henna red hair wasn't restrained in the usual braid but put up in a bun and decorated with an artificial rose. In her hand she had an envelope with something crackling inside.

My first impulse was to run away immediately, but she'd already seen me. I approached her with weak knees, my gaze fixed on her high-heeled shoes.

I asked if she had gotten lost.

"Only if you're lost up your own arse," she responded, and I noticed her lips were trembling.

"What are you doing here?" I asked, shifting my weight from one leg to the other. She hadn't come to school in quite a while, which had been a great relief to me. Now the bell was ringing for the end of the break, everyone was running to their classrooms and making a wide berth around Grandmother and me.

"Your Oma wants to offer her services," she said. "A ballet troupe. For all the fat girls at your school. You'll also take part."

At that moment the door to the office opened, and Grandmother floated inside. Appalled, I pulled a half-melted chocolate bar from my pants pocket and stuffed the whole thing into my mouth.

That afternoon Grandmother didn't come home. I didn't have a key, that way I couldn't lose it. I waited on the doormat in front of the locked door. Neighbors passed, newcomers, who gave me sympathetic glances and asked if I wanted their old children's books as their children were supposed to read German. But nobody offered to have me wait in their apartment.

Grandfather came home in the evening and let me in. Equally annoyed as I was, he searched the apartment for signs of Grandmother. Her suitcase was pulled out from under the cot, the lid open. Some certificates and documents had slid out of a brown envelope. I kneeled down and put out my hand, but Grandfather gathered everything together, shut the suitcase, and shoved it back under the bed. His secretive manner took away my desire to tell him about Grandmother's visit to the school.

I stayed on my knees and leaned down further, inhaling the dust of the too rarely cleaned corners. The unusual perspective puzzled me: it was new to me that under the cot wasn't just the suitcase but also various packages. I grabbed one of them and pulled it out, and my name in the address field sprang into my eye.

"This is for me?!" My hand reached for another package.

"Put it back." Grandfather's voice sounded dull, as if he was speaking into a bucket.

"But maybe all of them are for me?!"

"Get out of this room."

I was hurt. I was accustomed to being ordered about by Grandmother. Grandfather had never done anything like this before. In his dark gaze I felt like a piece of brittle, dried-out clay.

My stomach growled. I should have eaten and gone to bed long ago. Every deviation from the normal daily routine resulted in well-known health implications. Grandfather surveyed the contents of the refrigerator and the kitchen cabinets. I watched him. He hadn't even washed his hands beforehand.

We would starve miserably if Grandmother didn't show up soon.

"Noodles or buckwheat?" he asked over his shoulder in my direction. My stomach growled again. Noodles were an inferior food, only adults ate them because what they ate no longer mattered. But I was sick and tired of buckwheat.

"Noodles," I said.

A little while later Grandfather put a plate of spaghetti in front of me. It was a huge steaming mountain with a gigantic pat of butter in the middle. He held a ketchup bottle over my plate and looked at me inquisitively. I'd never been allowed to eat ketchup and nodded enthusiastically. Grandfather squirted a generous red trail on my mountain of noodles and stirred it up with a fork. I pounced on it, using my fingers to assist.

Grandfather sat opposite me, spinning his noodles onto his fork and smiling. I was fascinated by the sparing but also deft motion of his fingers, which were nearly black at the tips. The deep satisfaction of the moment made something in my stomach melt like a chocolate bar forgotten in a pocket.

Grandmother came home just after I had brushed my teeth. It was already late, and Grandfather made no attempt to check that I'd really managed to get all the spaces between the teeth clean. I ran into Grandmother, but she pushed me away and slumped into the chair.

Her lipstick and mascara were smeared and made her look simultaneously terribly sad and horribly funny. Despite my shock I was very careful not to burst out laughing. Her bun had fallen apart, strands of hair hung in her face. She took off one of her high-heeled shoes and threw it against the wall.

"Check my teeth, Grandma," I said in the hope that the familiar task would bring her back to our normality.

"Shut your mouth, they're going to rot anyway," she said. "Leave Oma alone, Maxim. Nobody wants the old lady. You hear that, Tschingis? Nobody. I might as well climb into a coffin and you can nail it shut."

Grandfather came closer and slowly fell to his knees.

"I used to be good, Tschingis! Do you remember?"

He took Grandmother's second shoe off and put it down carefully. He gently stroked her feet.

"The stupid cow of a director said I have no qualifications. I didn't want money from her, I just wanted to volunteer my knowledge to the school. Whatever Nina is doing I can do, too. A bit of piano, please, half of Russia plays piano, and all the Jews. The little cripple is getting bigger, he needs me less, I can start teaching, I said. When I stopped dancing I did stage design, that sheep of a school principal wouldn't even get a ticket to it, do you remember, Tschingis? And she said that if I have so much time on my hands I can sell cake at the summer festival."

"And what did you say?" I asked with a pounding heart.

"I put my name on the list," Grandmother said. "Do you stink of ketchup? Ketchup corrodes your esophagus."

DISGRACED WOMAN

O n the day of the summer festival, Grandmother got up at five. After her usual morning bathroom routine she disinfected her hands and put a spray bottle and wet wipes in her bag. She left unsalted cream of rice on the table for me and instructed Grandfather to check on my eating and then to bring me to the festival. Grandfather also got the task of watching over me and throwing me over the fence of the schoolyard at the slightest sign of danger. In my grandmother's eyes, large events were as risky as a flu epidemic, but she was too morally debilitated to fight over that, too, with Germany: "Fascists, what do you expect from them."

I would have far preferred to stay by myself in the apartment. Using a threadbare excuse I had in the presence of my grandparents squatted next to the cot, but the packages had disappeared. I asked myself if perhaps it had only been a dream.

The schoolyard was swarming with screaming children and balls flying around, and above the din came irregular cheers from the game stalls. But I could still hear Grandmother from a long way away. "Get in line!" she yelled. "Don't push! There's a million of you and I'm all by myself! That's your fourth piece, where are your parents? This coffee is too strong for someone your age, I'll add some milk. And sugar. Don't touch the cake, you haven't paid for it yet!"

Fortunately Grandmother yelled mostly in Russian. She looked spectacular: a short red dress offered a view of her muscular legs, her braid was coiled around her head and dazzlingly bright.

"Nina, my sunshine," thundered Grandmother's voice from the cake stand, and a shiver ran down my spine. "Help yourself to the last three pieces of crumb cake, you can get away with it with your figure. I'd give you the cake if it were mine, but it belongs to the community, and . . ." Grandmother paused as if someone had just muted her. As much as tried, I couldn't hear her anymore.

We walked home, the three of us, silent. I marveled at my forearm, dotted with stamps that I'd gotten at the various stands. It was sunny and warm, my T-shirt clung to my back. I relished the strange sensation of the evaporating moisture, something I'd rarely experienced in the past as Grandmother had tried to avoid my breaking out in a sweat. But now she wasn't paying any attention to me, while Grandfather probably wouldn't even have noticed if I'd lost my pants on the way home.

Lost in deep thought he carried the leftovers from the cake stand in tinfoil. Grandmother held a rose in her hand, a thank you to the volunteers that first generated girlish excitement in her only to quickly change into frustration.

"I made 243 rubles," she muttered as if she'd also baked all the cakes herself. "It was a slog. Nina is knocked up, Tschingis, did you see that?" She grabbed him on the arm and stopped him.

I saw the foil bundle slip out of his hands and went to try to catch it. But he was able to corral it himself at the last second, though his knuckles went white.

"She's old," said Grandmother. "She's . . . how old? Forty for sure. Older. In that case I could almost get pregnant again."

"You're not forty," I croaked from the side.

"And there are enough creatures on the earth," she interrupted me sharply. "Is the father present?"

I looked at Grandfather, unsure who the question was directed to.

"I thought so," said Grandmother more to herself.

I feared something bad would happen right there on the spot. I was surprised by Grandmother's discovery. Now I shared her distress, because I'd never experienced a child as grounds for happiness. But maybe Nina would be lucky and have a good, healthy baby, not a plague like me. The question of what Grandfather had to do with the whole thing was eating at the back of my mind, but I wouldn't let it make any further inroads.

"Poor woman," said Grandmother. "Being pregnant will make her ugly. Tschingis, be a good Christian and take the disgraced woman a sack of potatoes."

Nina's precarious condition had Grandmother on edge. When Grandfather had to go to a construction site on one of my piano days, she decided to accompany me to the lesson. I resisted mightily and assured her that, as an exception, I could make my own way to the piano lesson even in Grandfather's absence. Grandmother told a horrible story from her youth about a little boy and a tram. These days I easily recognized such stories as lies, and anyway Grandmother contradicted herself many times and transformed the original boy into a girl over the course of telling the story. To my surprise, however, this time she wouldn't be shaken off.

"What have you got there?" I asked in the tram, gesturing to two bulky plastic bags Grandmother wedged between us so they wouldn't be stolen by the other foreigners. She waved aside my question: "You wouldn't understand." She looked out the window and commented loudly about the clothing and distinctive features of people on the sidewalk. I would have liked to change seats. It occurred to me that something was happening that should never have been allowed to happen, and I thought despairingly of Grandfather, who hadn't made any arrangements for this situation and had left me alone to deal with his problems.

Suddenly I had a grand idea. The only catch was that it had occurred to me so late.

"We can't go there," I yelled as soon as the tram had stopped at a station. I jumped up, grabbed Grandmother by the hand, and pulled her out of the tram car. She grabbed frantically for the bags, stumbled, and cursed at me in a particularly refined fashion. I acted hurt even though I was celebrating inside.

"What's gotten into you?" she asked. "Do you need to go to the bathroom? Here in the bushes? I have newspaper here."

"No," I wheezed, still taken with my daring move. "I completely forgot that today there's no lesson."

"Why not?" Grandmother's eyebrows drew together to form an obtuse but grim angle.

"Nina is sick."

"Of course she's sick! You know what's wrong with her! A pregnancy like this is nothing at her age. I was twenty-seven, old for a first-time birth, and do you know how the doctor treated me? Like dirt. Why would I do this at my age, they asked me, and said that everyone would get sick, the mother, the child, nothing good would come of it. One doctor was nice, though, he told me straight away: You've done well, Margarita, you've basically hopped aboard the last wagon. For some people things go fine even at nearly thirty."

I said nothing, struck by the unwanted information.

"Tell me the address quickly," Grandmother ordered. "I bought buckthorn juice for Nina, she needs vitamins, she and her bastard."

"I don't have the address."

"I know you're an idiot, but you must know the address."

"I don't know it." I nearly started to cry. If I'd been able I would have taken out my idiocy and thrown it on the ground as evidence, or I'd have barked, just so she'd stop interrogating me.

"How do you always get there if you don't have any idea where it is?"

"Grandfather takes me," I muttered. The Soviet children's literature that my grandmother so treasured swarmed with brave partisans who wouldn't give up any secrets even under Nazi torture. Not even when the lives of their family members were on the line did important information pass their lips. I remembered my grandmother commenting at particularly disturbing passages: "You see, there used to be upstanding people. They had wills of steel. They weren't gobs of snot like you."

"What tram stop?" she asked now, and she began to take on the shape of a hangman. I blinked and saw Grandmother again, with her indignant eyebrows drawn together and vestiges of misguided eye shadow.

I closed my eyes with a sigh. I didn't want to be a gob of snot. But I didn't want to be tortured or threatened like the partisans, either. "One with trees. There's always people standing around."

"Aha. What else?"

"Then one block to the left. Or the right. And around another corner and three more blocks. The building is gray, with balconies."

My grandmother spat angrily on the ground. "Helpful as ever. Doesn't matter, I'll figure it out."

She didn't figure it out so quickly. The emergency lies that prevented at the last minute the encounter between Grandmother and Nina turned out to be prophetic. Nina canceled one piano lesson after the next. I didn't know if she was really doing that poorly or if she didn't want to see me anymore, and so I assumed it was a combination of the two.

Grandmother acknowledged every cancellation with a knowing nod.

She discussed Nina's bleak situation regularly with Grandfather. Every time I waited for the bomb to drop, for something to be said that would irretrievably cleave our life into two parts, one before and one afterward. But Grandfather's silence was ironclad. Once I even wondered if he wasn't actually cowardly rather than tight-lipped. He let my grandmother curse him as a heartless man if he didn't set out immediately to take Nina food and make sure she didn't need anything, water, medicine, lightbulbs. Oddly enough, she no longer tried to get to Nina either through him or through me, as if she had accepted our opposition even if she didn't understand it.

When Grandfather had to work at a construction site in the Harz for two weeks, Grandmother came home late one evening. She dropped onto the chair, unzipped the jacket of her tracksuit, and stretched out her legs, and in so doing hyperextended her feet in a way I couldn't even dream of doing. I asked her if I should take her shoes off for her. She held out first one foot and then the other.

"Where were you, Oma?" I asked after I'd placed her sneakers neatly in the foyer.

"Your Oma was slogging away," she said. "Unlike you all, I have a Christian heart. The poor woman was lying there in bed bloated, green in the face, and not a soul is looking after her."

"What? Who?" I asked, feeling a chill in my chest.

"Who else," said Grandmother. "That's how it is with us women. At first we're naïve and believe some shitty fellow. Then we're left alone with our problems."

"What did you do, Oma?" I asked hoarsely.

"Cleaned up is what I did! Her entire god damned apartment, on my knees like a *Neger*." She mimicked Nina: "*Please don't, please don't.* I told her: Nina, you already have an older child, you can't let yourself go. I'll help you, but you also have to do something yourself. When I was in your condition I even missed a transfusion and still went to work, at the theater. You can't prematurely declare yourself dead, Nina, I told her, a pregnancy ends at some point, but life goes on."

"You cleaned her whole place?" I asked, stunned.

"Do you think your Oma would only clean half?"

"Even the bathroom?" That's where my grandfather's toothbrush and razor were.

"The bathroom is the worst germ incubator in an apartment. If you don't keep it clean, you might as well just abandon the newborn baby in a dumpster."

"And did you open the wardrobes?"

"Should I have?" asked my grandmother. "Yes, I should have. Next time. You're an idiot, but sometimes wise."

That night she seemed happy and relaxed and even acted as if she didn't notice that I salted my mashed potatoes. She let me turn on the television. I sat down next to her on the couch and tried to concentrate on the plot of the crime story but gave up quickly. Grandmother asked after every scene who the people were and what they had just said. If there was no dialogue in the movie, she talked about the clothes and the furniture.

"Let's turn it off and go to sleep, I have a headache," I said.

"You see!" she said triumphantly. "Television rots your brain."

A Boy

By this time I'd managed to completely extricate Grandmother from all school business. I let invitations to parent-teacher nights slip by the wayside and signed everything that needed a signature from a legal guardian, scrawling it in Cyrillic, which eliminated any doubts the teachers may have had about the authenticity.

To my surprise, I was accepted at a good school, the same one as Vera. I nearly forgot to tell my grandparents that I was moving to another school. Grandmother still assumed that all German schools took ten years and that the upper grade students were taught in the same building as the lower grade students, just in the afternoons.

Switching schools felt as if a time machine had catapulted me back to the first year of school. We were the littlest ones again, I didn't know my way around the new school building, and had to figure out on my own which of the new students were out for my scalp.

Vera no longer left bruises and scratches on me anymore, but instead she never missed a chance to embarrass me, as if better times between us had never happened. She had sham laughing fits as soon as I raised my hand in class. When I was chosen and didn't immediately know the answer, she fed me the wrong answer, and I fell for it every time. She called me a butterball and a moron, made fun of my walk and accent, and told everyone that I had a crazy grandmother and took after her one hundred percent.

I let it all slide in the strong conviction that I had for some reason earned it. But after a few weeks I sought Vera out after class and grabbed her sleeve.

"Leave me alone," she said, pulling herself free, as if I was the one making her life difficult.

"It's not my fault," I said. "Do you understand? I can't do anything about it."

"It's *all* your fault," she said. "If you didn't exist, everything would be better."

"It is *not*!" I shouted.

"Whatever," said Vera. "We're moving anyway. I won't have to see you ever again."

"Moving where?" I asked, shocked.

"Like I'm going to tell you."

I realized she didn't know herself.

"When?"

"As soon as Mother is on her feet again," said Vera, and as a goodbye she kicked me in the shins, just like the good old days.

Our phone hardly ever rang. When Grandfather was away—and he was constantly away, building houses for other people for free, as Grandmother scowled because of his income—he didn't call home a single time. Some mornings Grandmother would freeze in the middle of a sentence and say: "What day is it? It's Uncle Fjodor's birthday," or "It's Soviet Army memorial day. One must congratulate all the men of the family." When I asked her why she never called anyone she reacted angrily: "Who's going to pay for that chitter chatter? You?"

Once or twice a year I witnessed the phone ring and Grandmother rushing to pick it up and yelling, "Hallo!" again and again until she finally said, "Fine, then," and hung up. The fact that the calls always came around my birthday and New

Year's, when all Russians congratulate their relatives, bothered me so much that I decided not to ask any questions.

Grandmother and I both cringed at night when the phone rang, the way we'd been taught to by television crime shows. It always meant somebody had been murdered. Grandfather was already in his cot on the other side of the wall, he had come home early by his standards.

I made it to the phone first.

"Hallo?" I said the way they did on TV. Grandmother came closer, I raised my gaze and saw Grandfather standing in the doorway unnaturally pale.

"Why are you crying, Vera?" I asked before Grandmother ripped the phone away from me.

"Dry your eyes now, child," she said. "I survived it, too, and your mother has broad hips. What did you say? How much water? Blood? Stop mumbling, I can't understand you. Put a towel beneath her. Is she conscious? So there you go. In that case it's not so bad. I'll send Opa over. He can take her to the hospital. Are you crying again? No, listen to me, she's not going to die. How is it my fault? You're dehydrated, dear child, and your mama probably is, too, the way she's howling in the background. You should both drink something. Old Margo will come over with Opa and bring you to our place. No you can't say that to your Oma, dear child, I don't know that word."

She hung up the phone and whirled around the apartment in a useless show of activity. Grandfather was still standing in the doorway, not moving. I wondered if someone could simultaneously be dead and standing up.

"Brainless man!" screamed Grandmother. "Do you have the car keys? The woman is deteriorating. Let's go!"

Later I believed Grandmother had been right and everyone really would have died without her. Amazingly quickly she returned with Vera. I'd stayed pressed to the window the whole time. I'd never been home alone so late at night before, in fact I was never left alone at all. I thought about using the opportunity to search the cabinets because I was still agitated about the packages that had disappeared. But my limbs felt as heavy as lead. When I finally decided to do it, it was too late.

Vera sat down next to me on the couch with glassy eyes, Grandmother set down the plastic bag she had hastily packed with Vera's things. "Old Margo has never left a child in a lurch," she said with satisfaction.

I shoved Vera's foot cautiously with the tip of my slipper. "Everything will be alright," I whispered. She didn't react.

"Shall I make you a fried egg with ketchup, dear child?" asked Grandmother.

"Where is his mother?" asked Vera in a monotone, gesturing at me.

"What did you say?"

"Where is his mother? Is it true that she sold him?"

"No," said Grandmother calmly. "Look at him, would anybody ask for money for that?"

Vera shook her head.

"There you go."

"But where is his mother then?"

I kicked Vera harder with my foot. Just because she felt rotten was no reason for her to drag other people down.

My grandmother's eyes flashed menacingly.

"Do you believe in a god, dear child?"

Vera shrugged her shoulders. "We're Jews."

"Doesn't matter. That happens. Go into the other room or somewhere else where nobody will see you, dear child, and kneel down and pray to your god. Perhaps he will help you and will be merciful to your beatific mama. And watch your filthy tongue in the future."

Vera got up and went into the other room. When I looked

in a bit later I found she was indeed on her knees. She was propped up on Grandfather's cot and murmuring something into her fists.

Grandfather came home shortly before sunrise. Grandmother and Vera had long since fallen asleep. Vera lay on a bed of pillows and blankets that Grandmother had put together on the floor. I was awake, listening to Grandmother's snores, with Vera's restless breathing as a second track. I heard the footsteps stop outside our door. Several minutes of silence followed, and I began to think I had misheard the steps. Then the key scraped into the lock and Grandfather crossed the room with quiet steps and faded into the darkness in the adjoining room. I slid off the couch and crept after him.

He sat down on the cot, his face buried in his hands. I sat next to him, nearly convinced that either Nina or the baby had died. I didn't know what I was supposed to say in situations like that. The question that animated me the most was whether Vera was now going to live with us forever, meaning Grandmother would then have the deadweight of two orphans to deal with. But I didn't dare blurt it out.

Grandfather took his hands away from his eyes. "Go to bed."

"We're all going to die," I said. I couldn't think of any better words of consolation.

He looked at me blankly. I didn't know what more I could say.

"A boy." Grandfather held his hands apart. "So tiny."

And only a few seconds later did I realize he wasn't talking about me.

MAZEL TOV

Grandmother didn't tell anyone when she headed off to the hospital with a helium balloon, a flower bouquet, and a cake. She came back with the exact same things, the balloon straining upward and bouncing behind her like a disobedient child. Vera and I were sitting at the table eating soup that Grandmother had made for us in the gray first light of morning and left on the windowsill.

"You couldn't find the hospital?" I asked hopefully.

"The stupid woman isn't there anymore," said my grandmother. "She took off, the nut, and nobody was able to stop her."

"They're not allowed to," said Vera. Ever since she'd found out her mother hadn't died, she had been very concerned about her basic rights again. As Grandmother had already observed a few times, the German language had unpleasantly stained her: Vera always wanted to debate things, an example I was explicitly not to follow. About her little sibling Vera conspicuously did not ask.

"Hospitals are allowed to confine mothers who pose a threat to their child," said Grandmother. "Where can she be? In a shelter for disgraced girls? She hasn't been a girl in thirty years."

"Maybe she's at home," I said, and under the table Vera gave me the hardest kick I'd felt up to now.

When we later talked about whose fault all of what followed was, Vera put all the blame on me. If I hadn't put that stunning thought in Grandmother's head, our lives, in Vera's opinion, would have gone on unchanged, two parallel existences that never intersected, with me as the only go-between.

What happened, however, was that the three of us climbed aboard the tram. Vera and I carried between us a plastic bag with tiny rompers that Grandmother had sought out in secondhand shops, then washed and ironed them. The helium balloon was already wilting and kept bumping against Grandmother's head, which we would have found funny in other circumstances. Now, though, neither Vera nor I was in any mood to laugh. We scuffed our feet in front of Grandmother as the treetops rustled and the wind carried a sweet scent of blossoms mixed with something decaying. Grandmother kept shoving us in the back. My shin still hurt terribly. I peered over at Vera, her face was blank, as if someone had turned out the light.

We saw Nina and Grandfather from a long way away. They were standing in the entryway of the building, and Nina, whom I hadn't seen in months, seemed both bloated and thinner at the same time, pale and infinitely tired. Between her and Grandfather was a bulky stroller that was draped with a white scarf. The wind buffeted the scarf as well as the balloon, the string of which Grandmother clutched.

She didn't seem surprised to find Grandfather next to Nina. She gave me and Vera final instructions: "Keep your distance from the newborn. Any germ could kill the baby. You two are filthy bacteria slings. You should lie down," she transitioned seamlessly to address Nina. "Why are you holding her up with your nonsensical chatter, Tschingis? You want the milk to go bad?"

She leaned down over the stroller and lifted the white scarf. Against her instructions, Vera and I immediately crowded in behind her to get a look. I'd never seen a newborn before. I was of the same opinion as my grandmother, that they should be kept behind closed doors in sterile conditions for the first few weeks.

Lying in the stroller, wrapped in a blanket, was the tiniest being I'd ever seen. It was so little that it didn't even seem human to me. It must have come from another world, from some alien workshop, where they'd crafted an exquisite miniature copy of my grandfather.

Vera and I were standing side by side next to the stroller when we noticed Grandmother had taken a step back. Vera put out her hand and touched the baby on the ear, and I wanted to shout at her not to break anything. I turned to Grandmother. Without looking at her face, I took her hand after I'd confirmed that Grandfather had taken the flowers and the bag from her. I hadn't thought about the balloon, and it followed us, buffeted by the wind, to the tram stop, where Grandmother finally let go of my hand.

"Do you want to lie down, Oma?" I asked once we were safely home. Grandmother hadn't said a single word during the ride. I would have preferred it if she'd dumped the contents of her purse over my head and cursed the entire world. In order to keep her busy I'd asked her nonsense questions the whole time, like whether the Soviet flag really got its red color from the blood of our enemies, and whether I'd ever be able to taste French fries, and finally even if she'd ever fallen off the stage during her past as a dancer. Grandmother hadn't reacted.

At home, too, I'd not been able to catch her gaze even once. I pulled out the couch, pinching my finger in the process, just as Grandmother had always predicted, and shouted: "Ouch!" But none of it seemed to interest her. I got out the bedclothes and spread them out on the couch as best I could, and fluffed the pillows. Grandmother sat motionless at the table. I took her a glass of water, then, after a bit of thought, a glass of vodka. The bottle was in the refrigerator, Grandmother believed in vodka poultices in the case of fever. Finally I shook her arm.

"Leave your Oma alone, little one," came a murmur from her mouth. I looked at Grandmother. Before me sat an old lady shriveled like the balloon we'd bought for Nina.

I choked back my tears and put on the television. She still didn't say a word.

I didn't expect Grandfather to come home that night. For all intents and purposes, I thought, he didn't ever need to come back. There was nothing here that he would need urgently. His toothbrush was at Nina's. His miniature copy as well. I could sleep on his cot tonight. On the other hand, could I really leave Grandmother alone on the couch in her condition?

While I was in the bathroom I heard the apartment door open and then close again. I was sure that Grandmother was heading for the nearest river. She had talked of that time and time again in desperate moments: "I can't take it any longer with you two. Where's the nearest river?" And it played no role that the nearest river was thirty kilometers away and that she had no driver's license. But when I had a look, she was still sitting there. Sitting opposite her was Grandfather. Their hands were on the table but not touching, and the strange peacefulness of the scene tickled my nose. I fought off an urge to sneeze.

"You know, Tschingis, dear Maya," said my grandmother after what felt like an eternity. "Not a day goes by when I don't think of her. I know the same is true for you. It'll continue as long as we live. This cripple here," she gestured in my direction with her head, "he's here for life, too. You can't leave him behind, and at some point you'll be all alone with him. Every year counts double for me. I'm an old woman, and you're a young man. I'm sorry that you made another brat, but that baby has a mother and this one here does not. He has no one except us."

She paused for a long time, inhaling deeply. Then she

reached across the table, pulled the open pack of cigarettes from the breast pocket of my grandfather's shirt, and took a lighter from the shelf above her head. She lit a cigarette and, with excited horror, I inhaled the smoke wafting towards me into lungs that had supposedly been clotted since my birth. In our apartment there'd been a strict no smoking policy as long as I could remember.

"Your punishment is us, Tschingis," said my grandmother. "Look your Margo in the eyes. I'm not going to hold you back, you are a free man. You work a lot, your honor isn't at issue. So you have a son. It fills one with pride: A son. Go to him if you want to. And think of dear Maya. Perhaps she'd still be alive if . . ."

My grandmother put the cigarette out in a coffee cup.

"Congratulations, Tschingis," she said after another pause. "I forgot to say that in all the excitement. You'll have to forgive me. Mazel tov."

I leaned against the wall because I was suddenly overwhelmingly tired. Grandfather sat upright, tears ran down his dark cheeks. I couldn't stand the sight. At that same moment I stopped trying to suppress a fit of coughing, and my lungs exploded.

LITTLE UNCLE

I t wasn't the sound of a baby screaming that woke me, because, in my deep sleep, I just incorporated the screaming into something unrelated to me, like the static from the television next door, on the other side of my thin wall. It was the much softer hissing of my grandmother that woke me with a start. I sat up in bed immediately, rubbed my eyes, and let myself fall back onto the pillows once I'd remembered that it wasn't due to me this time. For outsiders the sound might have seemed threatening, but I knew the differences in the noises my grandmother made.

"Shshsh," she'd say persistently and affectionately while swaying gently back and forth on the chair. She'd thrown a scarf over the lamp on the nightstand, which did dull the light but also cast spooky shadows on the wall. The milk gurgled from the bottle, the baby sighed. I closed my eyes.

"Good boy," purred my grandmother. "No need to cry so loudly, you see you've woken Maxi. Maxi needs to go to school in the morning so he doesn't stay so stupid. You're a big boy, you're seven months old now, you'll go to school, too, and bring the best grades home to old Margo."

I was no longer awake when she went back to the couch. The baby still slept in a cardboard moving box that served as a provisional bed for him. Grandfather wasn't there.

"Back at the construction site, the wretch," murmured Grandmother. "Takes every job just to get out of the house. As soon as the baby arrives the wife's no longer any fun, eh?"

When I tried to ponder how it was that we had a baby in the apartment now, I just couldn't. I tried to remember that moment immediately after the birth of my uncle, when Grandfather stood motionless at the window as if Nina still lived on the other side of the courtyard, but actually never saw the children of the newcomers at play because he had his eyes shut. I remembered Grandmother and the growing tension she spread, and how she dropped things one after the next, a spoon, an apple, a plate. She never picked them up. At some point she sent Grandfather out with a shopping list. He came home with diapers and groceries.

My grandparents carried full bags to Grandfather's car and disappeared for a few hours. I stayed behind with the unfamiliar feeling of being forgotten. After they returned Grandmother held forth about which types of cribs were particularly deadly. A day later my grandparents carried a large carton to the car together, and Grandmother told me that Grandfather had put together a crib under her guidance. Finally she held out her palm to Grandfather and ordered him to hand over the key to Nina's apartment. I couldn't see his face, but he obeyed.

That same day Grandmother came home as white as a cadaver.

"I bought her vitamins," she muttered, bracing herself on my shoulder. "I rang the bell politely, and only afterwards opened the door. Nobody was there. The refrigerator was empty, the trash was full. Didn't I tell you to look in them every day, you Asian gob?! Why do you screw everything up? What will I do now?"

I found myself torn between the desire to run away and the nearly inexorable pull of the pain Grandmother was screaming in Grandfather's direction.

"She's weak, she can't get far, Margaritalein," said Grandfather hoarsely.

"Where do you think she is now? How many disgraced women have been fished out of the river with their bastard child?"

"There's no river around here . . . ," I muttered, but it wasn't heard.

"Call the police!"

"And Vera was at school this morning," I said. This time I was heard, and Grandmother abruptly calmed down.

It was easier than it seemed: Grandmother needed only follow Vera after school the next day. Nina had checked into a cheap hotel in the city and screamed at my grandparents to get out of her life. Grandmother swore that Nina would have thrown the baby at her if she hadn't grabbed it in time.

She settled the hotel bill, took Nina, Vera, and the baby back to the apartment and left money and food for them. A little later she went back again and took the baby with her. Nina was lying in bed and didn't react.

Against his normal practice, Grandfather opened his mouth and asked whether they should get a doctor. Grandmother shook her head. "She's gone nuts, don't you see that? Do you know what they do with the mentally ill? If she's committed you'll never see her again."

Ever since, my uncle has lived in the moving box at our place because according to Grandmother, when faced with the suggestion that the crib be transported to our place, Nina "had acted irrational." For years afterwards, I never understood why in those weeks Nina gave up her child but not the crib. Grandmother went over to Nina's daily to collect the mother's milk she pumped, and scolded her for her lack of diligence in this matter. Nina lay with her face to the wall. She didn't react as Grandmother sterilized the bottles and held forth on the feeding of infants. "Hygiene is everything, Nina. Look at Maxi. His intestinal flora was completely ruined. It cost me may years of my life to reestablish it." It surprised me that she spoke of me now in the past tense, as if I was no longer a problem case and could live, eat, and breathe like a normal person. Nina didn't stir.

Grandmother had less and less time for me, too. Only seldom did I find boiled and pureed dishes made just for me. Grandmother was too busy with the care of the baby and with transporting the precious drops of mother's milk through the city. She took to cursing only in a sweet, high-pitched tone.

"How can Tschingis stand it?" asked Vera at school when I nodded asleep into my notebook because the baby had woken up all night again only to be fed and shushed to sleep by Grandmother. For a fraction of a second I wondered if she meant my grandfather or the baby. I found it annoying to use the same first name for such an old person and such a young one. Grandmother also hadn't been pleased with the name selection, after all my grandfather wasn't even dead, and there was no need to mess up the kid's life right from the start by giving him a slit-eyed name. But Nina had refused to even consider Grandmother's suggestion—Boris. With the registration of the name, Nina had presented it to everyone as a done deal.

I liked the fact that Grandmother's new problems had nothing to do with me and she sometimes seemed to forget that I even existed. Vera seemed less happy with the changes. She had grown so much in the past few months that even I noticed despite the fact that I saw her every day. Her pants were suddenly tighter and her ankles were visible, her arms stuck out of her sleeves, and even her expressions seemed to have changed: her once round, brown eyes were now narrow and skeptical, and her lower lip had become fuller and more sullen.

"How can Tschingis stand it?" Vera repeated, and this time I wondered about the arrogance it took for her to refer to my grandfather by his first name.

"He's good at suffering through," I muttered. Grandfather was the only one who hadn't changed. Only the palms of his hands had gotten softer, even if the skin was peeling in several places.

"Wash your hands!" yelled Grandmother every time as soon as Grandfather returned home from his construction site. "Wait, I'll come with you, you never really learned to do it properly, you didn't even have toilet paper growing up. You scrub for such a short amount of time? It doesn't surprise me. You need more foam. Look how black the soap is. You wanted to touch the baby like that? With all that construction grime? Soap up again. See, better, the foam's gray. Again. Dry off well. Hold out your hands. The rough stuff's gone, but without disinfectant there are still germs." I heard the hiss of the spray.

Grandfather sat down on a chair holding little Tschingis. In his free time he no longer lay on the cot, he sat for hours and stared at his son's face.

"Does he look like me?" I asked one afternoon when my lunch had been completely forgotten and I'd made myself a fried egg and two for Grandmother.

"Nonsense," said Grandmother. "He looks like your grand-father."

"But I look like Grandfather. You call me Asian gob, too."

"I'd never say something like that." Grandmother kissed the baby's dark tuft of hair, stealthily rubbed the spot with a boiled cloth, and muttered: "Thank god I don't have herpes."

"What did I look like as a baby?" I asked.

"Like the most annoying child in the world, which you became, too," my grandmother exploded. "Am I supposed to remember everything? What's with the family history? If you're itching so much with curiosity go look in the suitcase and compare yourself."

She didn't have to tell me twice. I ran into the adjoining room, fell to my knees, and pulled the suitcase out from under the cot. I carried it with surprising ease back into the living room and dropped it on the couch. The latch, too, was laugh-ably easy to open.

I shoved aside the heavy clothes, carefully put the worn-out ballet slippers on the floor, and pulled out the thick envelope where the photos and documents were stored. Inside was a smaller envelope, I'd never been permitted to touch it because the negatives of the photos were lost and my hands destroyed everything they touched.

I spread the photos out in front of me like a card game. One photo showed a crying child on the potty who was so ugly that it could only have been me. In another one was my grandfather in a soldier's uniform, next to him a bride whom I recognized as the somewhat more mature version of the swan from the ballet photo. My grandmother smiled at the camera and seemed perfectly happy. Grandfather was somewhat thinner than now and had smoother skin. But I couldn't spot any more serious changes despite all the decades.

In another picture he was holding little Tschingis in his arms. The image stung me, because there were no photos of me and Grandfather, only one of me and Grandmother where she was holding me on a swing. I must have been two or three and looked panicky, covered except for my eyes in a fur coat, hat, and scarf.

I picked up another photo that I had a hard time deciphering. It showed a girl in a Soviet school uniform, and since it was yellowed like the others were, I assumed from the facial features that it was of a sister of my grandfather. I didn't know anything about his family. Grandmother always hinted that Grandfather hadn't had running water or electricity during his childhood, and that the powerful hand of civilization only reached him in the saving form of Grandmother.

"Who's this girl, Oma?" I asked.

"Quiet!" She was standing in the doorway rocking little Tschingis in her arms. "Don't worry, my little treasure, everyone yells here like in the forest. Grandmother might be old, but she's not deaf."

She leaned over my shoulder and got very quiet. "Maya," she said, not to me but to the photo.

"Dear Maya?"

"Dear Maya," echoed Grandmother.

"Aha," I said. "Why is the picture of Opa and little Tschingis also so yellow?" I held the photo out to her.

"That's not little Tschingis, idiot. That's Maya, too. All of your grandfather's children look like carbon copies."

"If not for Maya, Grandfather wouldn't be here anymore," I suddenly said as if someone had whispered the sentence in my ear.

"If not for Maya, none of us would be here," said Grandmother dully.

The words floated past me, and I didn't even want to think about them. But then they turned, just as the wind sometimes changes direction, and they bored their way into my brain.

"If not for Maya, I wouldn't exist at all," I said and wished so badly that Grandmother would correct me. But Grandmother looked at the photo and nodded again and again as if she were talking to it.

"Why did you never tell me?" I asked, fighting rising disappointment because it became clear to me at that moment that in my mind Maya, too, had been a blonde princess with soft features and delicate hands.

"What?"

"Why didn't you ever tell me outright that Maya's my mother?"

"So confused, the boy, all the hormones," Grandmother complained impassively to the girl in the photo. "Now he's constantly accusing me, the old lady is always at fault, how convenient. What was I supposed to have told him instead? Who was his mother supposed to be, Mary Poppins?"

I turned away, I didn't want to see her or her photos. At the same time I feared Grandmother would never stop being right. She was even right when she was wrong. She knew me better than any other person, and she knew something about this world that nobody else had a clue about.

*

Grandmother steadfastly refused to talk more about Maya. She continued to insist that her heart would conk out if she did.

"What happened to her?" I pushed anyway. "Who killed her?"

"Shut your filthy mouth. Divert yourself by doing something useful. Go out, take the tram, look in on Nina."

"You look in on her."

"Listen, my little piece of gold, to how this little freak talks about your good-for-nothing mother. He's not entitled to talk that way, even if she doesn't deserve any better."

"Why won't you tell me?!" I lost control.

"Don't shout in here, boy, you're not in the forest. I know the hormones are beginning to rage in you, but I'm old and deserve respect. I've invested so many years of my life in you, and now what's come of that is an ungrateful swine who inconsiderately shouts awake a little angel."

"He does the same thing to me."

"Because he doesn't know any better, do you understand, birdbrain?"

"I understand plenty," I say, suddenly calm again. "You can't let him out of your hands because the baby looks like Maya."

The silence that descended made it feel as if somebody had put a pillow over my face. My grandmother's look reduced me to ashes. And while I collapsed inside, I continued to stare at her face. "What happened to Maya, Oma," I said. "What did you do with her?"

She began to sob and turned her broad back to me. She held little Tschingis tighter. He looked at me over her shoulder. For a moment I forgot my cares, lost pondering whether he could already recognize me. I wished I'd never heard Grandmother whisper, "It was Opa."

THE SWORD

I had my hands full of henna at the moment the doorbell rang. For a while now I'd had the honor of helping Grandmother dye her hair. At first I'd been fascinated as I watched the way she stirred boiling water into the brown powder, poured in a touch of red wine, and covered the floor of the bathroom with newspapers. She had a comb and brush at the ready for me, sat down on a stool, and took the hair tie out of her braid.

The braid was already immensely long. When it was unbraided the hair was even longer, and in the light of the bathroom lamp it shone bright red with silver shimmering roots.

Grandmother combed her hair with a coarse-pronged comb. She smeared the skin at the roots with Vaseline so it wouldn't take on the hair color. I put on rubber gloves, picked up the brush, and went through the heavy hair strand by strand.

At first she yelled at me constantly because she suspected I wasn't working carefully enough and just wanted to get through the job as quickly as possible. But that wasn't true: I liked tasks that consisted of the endless repetition of small, simple steps. I felt like a painter who just had to make a few last strokes before his work achieved perfection. I loved dipping the silver hair in henna, the brown goop stunk like a swamp and gave me the feeling of being part of a magic ritual.

I had just finished the left side of the head when the doorbell rang. It was Saturday, and Grandfather was out with little Tschingis getting some fresh air and giving Grandmother a chance for beauty care. I took off my right glove and went with the brush in my left hand to the door.

I'd last seen Nina shortly after little Tschingis's birth. I'd nearly forgotten that she used to live here in this complex, too. I wondered why her light blue eyes had once seemed so warm to me. Her empty and exhausted gaze took in the smeared kitchen apron that was supposed to protect my clothes from henna stains. The momentary irritation made her look for a split second like the Nina who had once taught me soldiers' songs at Grandmother's request.

"Where is he?"

"Taking a walk," I said, assuming she meant my grandfather. Nina took a step to the side, and I saw that she wasn't alone. Behind her stood a woman in jeans and a leather jacket with short blonde hair and a little tear tattoo on her temple, who calmly shoved her foot into the doorway when I went to close it.

I was pushed aside with embarrassing ease, and Nina stepped into our apartment with her new acquaintance. The leather-jacketed woman crossed the room in a few steps. She gestured to Tschingis's freshly washed romper drying on the laundry line my grandfather had strung across the room. The boiled milk bottles stood upside-down on a sterilized wash-cloth on the kitchenette counter.

"Anytime soon?" Grandmother, who had already shown an uncharacteristic degree of patience, called from the bathroom. "The only thing you can be sent out to get is one's death!"

The stranger picked up a baby rattle from the couch with a meaningful look, pressed it into Nina's hand, and opened the bathroom door. The view of my grandmother, with half of her head covered with a greenish mass, left her stunned. For a moment it seemed as if she wanted to excuse herself, but then she said: "Where's the baby?"

Grandmother squinted, with her glasses set aside because of the dyeing process. "Do I know you, dearest?" she asked in her most friendly Russian.

The stranger turned to Nina: "What is she saying?"

"Please be so kind as to leave my bathroom, particularly in outdoor shoes," Grandmother continued before Nina could open her mouth.

"I won't put up with it any longer, Margarita Ivanovna," said Nina with a frail voice. "Give me my son back and we can part ways in peace."

"I can't follow the conversation," whispered the leather-jacketed stranger.

"What's the lesbian saying, Maxi?"

"You can't do this, Margarita Ivanovna. You are . . . you were a mother yourself."

"Burglar! Police!" yelled my grandmother.

The voices crackled in my ear. I noticed that Nina seemed more exhausted by the minute, she was already leaning against the wall. In the middle of the chaos I heard with relief my grandfather, who must have just come through the door: "Rita dear, he's wet!"

Nina, the leather-jacketed stranger, and I pushed our way out of the bathroom, leaving Grandmother on her stool. Grandfather was standing there holding little Tschingis in outstretched arms waiting for a helping female hand. Although he hadn't reckoned on Nina's appearance, he smiled happily when he saw her. At that moment I understood that I still had no clue about the adult world.

"Look, Mommy's here!" said Grandfather, handing the baby to Nina. "Finally she's back with us. Didn't I tell you? They always come back, mommies."

Nina squeezed her son to herself, and little Tschingis let out a deafening scream of protest. Grandmother appeared with a towel over her shoulders.

"You came here with a sword?" she said to Nina. "Got it. From now on you can get by on your own. I don't want to see you or him," her voice trembled as she gestured toward the baby, "ever again."

From that day until her next hair-dye session two weeks later, she walked around with silver shimmers on the right side of her head that reminded me of a halved halo.

Every time Grandfather took a turn a little too sharply, Vera let herself purposefully fall over onto me. I sat between her and her mother, bathed in sweat that was running from the roots of my hair down my neck and back, some of it oozing into the waistband of my pants and some of it dripping down my calves into my sandals.

I did everything I could to avoid letting Vera's body cause me to bump into Nina, and knew that I'd have sore muscles the next day from the effort. The air conditioning in Grandfather's old VW had never worked, and Grandmother always opened the window just a tiny crack, and even that for only a few minutes. Drafts had been the cause of many children's demise, and Tschingis was a weak if genial one-year-old. If anything happened to him it really would be a shame, unlike with some other babies.

He was sitting in my lap, which according to Grandmother was the safest place in the car for an infant. The belt pressed us together, and I worried that we might be forever stuck together with sweat if we were to stay this way while driving through Austria and France all the way to the Spanish coast. Before we passed the abandoned border checkpoints a light scarf was thrown over Tschingis because Grandmother suspected the Europeans might jump out of the bushes and demand proof that the baby was ours. In my opinion the family resemblance was obvious, but nobody listened to me. The fact that Tschingis stayed quiet at these moments was taken by Grandmother as further proof of his genial nature.

She didn't believe in child seats, and Nina had admitted defeat on this issue astonishingly quickly. Any other seating arrangement would have meant we were one spot short, and the journey together wouldn't have been possible.

Grandfather didn't say a word during the entire drive, which had nothing to do with the driving conditions. When we stopped at a rest stop, he did some exercises and took hard-boiled eggs and pickles from Grandmother's hand. Once in a while, on her orders, he sat down in the shade and closed his eyes to gather energy for the rest of the drive. Grandmother viewed steering a car as most demanding work, requiring appropriate attention and also rest. For this reason Grandfather was relieved of looking after genial Tschingis during the breaks. Nina and Grandmother took turns watching over him, so that the other could go, armed with disinfectant spray, to the bathroom. Vera and I were given the tasks of not being a burden on anyone and behaving in a way so as to be invisible. Unlike Vera, I accomplished this easily until we finally reached our hotel.

Grandmother had booked the accommodations after she'd found a pamphlet in our mailbox. "The children need to get to the seaside," she'd told Grandfather. "It's too late for Maxi, but Tschingis will be rickety otherwise. His brain is still developing. Do you remember, Maxi, how you were put under UV lights at the polyclinic as a toddler so your bones didn't get too weak? Didn't help. Too little sun is simply too little sun."

Now she sat on her lounge chair beneath a large hat every day. Unlike us she wasn't afraid of sunburn, which is why she refused to put on sunblock. She was bronze by the third day.

Me, on the other hand, I had a bright red back on the first day already, and the next morning the skin had begun to peel. Grandmother realized the extent of the damage immediately and sent Grandfather to the breakfast buffet to get yoghurt.

He had to go back a second time because the first time he brought fruit-flavored yoghurt. Nina and Vera stood by my bed as Grandmother spread the cool goop around my back with her fingers. I felt with horror that her fingers were trembling.

"It's okay, Oma," I said. The trembling got worse. A big glob landed on my shoulder and an even bigger one on the pillow. I twisted my arm and wiped up the yoghurt with a finger and licked it off.

"It's not so bad," I whispered.

It was Vera who caught the half empty yoghurt container that fell from my grandmother's hand. Grandmother slumped sobbing to the floor, hammering on the threadbare carpet with her fists.

"What have I done!" she screamed into the barely visible pattern of the carpet.

"I'm fine!" I yelled, but she didn't seem to hear me.

I jumped up, the yoghurt tickling me as it ran down my back. Together we mustered the strength to lift Grandmother and put her on the bed. Nina and I each held one of her hands because she was now trying to scratch her own face.

"It's just a measly sunburn!" shouted Vera.

Grandmother raised her head noisily. She stood up, went unsteadily into the bathroom, and straightened her hair. Vera sat down next to me, breathing heavily. I realized that she'd been overwhelmed by the scene and put my arm around her. She moved closer to me and leaned her head on my shoulder, and now we were both covered in yoghurt. Nina looked at us shaking her head.

I had expected Grandmother to follow my every step with a bottle of sunscreen after that, but I was wrong: she only half-heartedly reminded me to stay in the shade and keep a T-shirt on. Most of the time she stretched out in her beach chair next to Nina. From a distance it looked as if the two of them were engrossed in a discussion, but I didn't believe that impression. Nina looked as if somebody had sucked out all her previous warmth and buoyancy, and for reasons that were incomprehensible to me, I feared I was at fault for it. I remembered unhappily the moment when, a few weeks after she'd taken Tschingis back and Grandmother had fallen into despair, she was suddenly at our apartment door again, crying. For some reason I was the one who opened the door. Months later I couldn't shake the feeling that I could have changed something if I'd only managed to find the right words at that moment, but Grandmother suddenly came up behind me and stretched out her arms for little Tschingis. I wondered why one of the two of them always had to be unhappy whenever the other one wasn't.

The past few weeks seemed to have been a good time for Grandmother.

"Just no preschool, Nina," she lectured from her beach chair, one leg crossed atop the other. "Is our boy an orphan? Margo is here, she'll take care of everything. When I said before that the devil should take you and rip you into bits and roast you, I meant it in a loving way." I didn't catch Nina's answer; for the most part she just held her book tightly.

I suggested to Vera that we build a sandcastle for Tschingis. Vera followed me grudgingly. We went far enough away that Grandmother could still see us but we could no longer hear her.

"So boring," said Vera as I dug out the moat of the castle. "Why do we have to stick around here? Can't two old women manage to look after one little child on their own?"

"No idea."

"And anyway, your grandfather is here, too."

Grandfather sat a bit off to the side reading a newspaper beneath a palm tree. Sometimes he lay beneath a palm tree and slept.

"Leave him be," I said.

"Will you be like that, too?" asked Vera.

I shrugged and then took off my T-shirt. Vera moved closer. "Doesn't look bad at all, your sunburn."

"My grandmother knows her way around emergencies."

"Why don't you ever defend yourself? Against anyone?"

I couldn't come up with anything.

At the breakfast buffet Grandmother eyed the plates that other hotel guests were carrying to their tables critically and assessed their selection and portion sizes. Once she followed a French vacationer through the entire room to ask whether he really needed five slices of watermelon and whether her children should starve on his behalf. She called him a fascist and returned to our table with his plate.

"Don't touch it," she said. "He breathed on it."

"Why did you take it away from him then?" I asked.

"It's a matter of principle, Maxi."

From then on Vera and I tried to avoid the group breakfast. While Vera just ignored the grandmotherly directions, I pretended that the buffet made my stomach sick. Grandmother nodded with satisfaction and from then on made me gruel every morning in a toothbrush cup with the help of an immersion heater. Most of the time I was able to duck into the breakfast room on the way to the beach and secretly gulp down some leftover pieces of cake. Despite the gruel, I enjoyed the ten days at the seaside because everyone except Nina seemed to be in a good mood.

On the day of our departure, of all days, Grandmother overslept. I woke up before her, she lay snoring on the double bed she was sharing with me, while Grandfather had gotten the portable cot, though I'd never seen him sleeping on it. Today, too, he was already gone, supposedly he took long walks on the beach or sat with a cup of tea at the bar. I shifted

Grandmother's braid off her face so she could breathe better. Then I hopped into my pants and ran down to the dining room, relishing a last chance to have breakfast undisturbed by Grandmother.

I was pleased to find Grandfather and Vera at our table. Grandfather had Tschingis in his lap and was feeding him cornflakes. I sat down next to him.

"My mother says that in your culture lots of men had multiple wives," said Vera with her mouth full, without acknowledging my presence. Apparently the conversation was going to continue for a while.

Grandfather took a sip of tea. The teabag was still in the cup. I stared at it the whole time, tormented by the desire to pull it out, as my grandmother would have done immediately. Unlike Vera, I knew she wouldn't get an answer. This time I found that a shame. I didn't have the slightest hint about my grandfather's culture, and it began to dawn on me that I'd missed out on something important.

"Where's Nina?" I asked.

"Mama and Margarita Ivanovna got drunk last night." Vera said it casually, but seemed ready to pounce on my reaction.

"Not funny," I said.

"Not a joke. They were at the hotel bar together. Mama stumbled into bed at nearly dawn."

"Don't talk about your mother that way," said Grandfather. Vera choked on her hot chocolate and started to cough.

Grandmother suddenly popped up behind Vera and clapped her hard between her shoulder blades. She must have just braided her hair but she looked unkempt, as if she'd just rolled out of bed, and yet she seemed to be in a bright mood. "Dear girl, move over a little. Save yourself the poisonous glare, I don't even see it. Tschingis, listen. The woman thinks I should open a dance school. At my age! Crazy, right? What do you think?"

"What? Who?" Vera and I asked at the same time as Grandfather got up to get Grandmother a glass of orange juice.

"It's the craziest thing, right Tschingis?" Grandmother held his sleeve and tried to look him in the eyes. "Do the Germans have any knowledge whatsoever of beauty and elegance? I don't think so."

Grandfather put the orange juice down in front of her. He looked as if he was solving a complicated math problem in his head.

"Where's my mother?" asked Vera.

"How should I know? She can't drink, dear girl. I don't know why she insists on doing it anyway. Maxi, go to the room, pack your bag, I'm not your slave. Take this little treasure here and wash out his sweet mouth. We're leaving in an hour."

On the way home Nina had a green face and three times she asked Grandfather to stop. She didn't manage to make it to the bathroom and threw up twice in the bushes and once on the side of the road. Without comment, Grandmother handed her disinfectant and a thermos with hot water. Grandfather looked off into the distance, probably to avoid embarrassing Nina.

"Sometimes I think my mother is married to your grandmother," Vera whispered in my ear.

"No, they hate each other," I said, as if that would rule out marriage.

Do not Speak with Red-Haired Strangers

Back home Grandmother suddenly began again to warn me again about strangers who might try to talk to me on the street. Sometimes it was gypsies, sometimes American pederasts, once in a while Chinese organ dealers, but whoever it was, things always ended badly.

Even so, I already had the impression that despite herself Grandmother had begun to relax. She was amazed that a man who looked Mediterranean had brought one of the neighbor's children back to the home in top health after finding the child on the street, lost. Another person, who likewise had traces of a violent ethnicity in his face, had gone to great pains to bring back Grandmother's wallet, which she had left somewhere while shopping and had complained it had been underhandedly stolen. He'd turned down a reward as well as a package of chocolates, and Grandmother couldn't get over it for days: "An Arab, and yet upstanding." During this time she stopped locking the door every night with a chain.

When she suddenly started again to warn me, I tried to act dumb: "What if the stranger just asks for directions?"

"Get away. Especially if he knows you name."

"How could a stranger know my name?"

"How should I know?" Despite all the practice she was still not a good liar.

"What if it's a woman?"

"It won't be a woman. Definitely not with you. In any case, just get away."

"But then she'd think I was weird."

"She'll think that either way."

"And what if she says I've inherited a million?"

Grandmother's facial expression irritated me. I'd already forgotten a little what it was like when she worried about me.

"What does he look like, your stranger I'm not to answer?" I asked placatingly.

She avoided looking at me. "I don't know what he looks like now."

"Now? What did this guy used to look like?"

"I've forgotten."

"You never forget anything."

"Red hair," said my grandmother wearily. "Nose. Glasses. Ugly as the night. Leave me alone, I really don't know anything more."

Meanwhile the phone was ringing constantly at our place. The time when we would cringe at the sound was long gone. The phone sat on the nightstand next to the couch so Grandmother needed only reach out her hand to answer it.

"How old?" she asked over the phone. "Three? She'll cry. Four? She'll cry, too. You can come, the first lesson is free. One-year contract. No, not month to month. If that's the way it is at the German ballet school take your child there. All the fat Turkish girls are there, in pink tutus. If that's what you want. I've warned you at no charge. With me, three times a week. Yes, even at four years old. Anyone who doesn't come regularly won't have any right to a role in the Nutcracker. And kindly console your child yourself in that case."

Shortly after getting home from Spain she'd discovered a space next to the new Russian supermarket. A produce shop had just gone out of business. Grandmother had tracked down the owner and gotten a fixed lease. Grandfather renovated the space exactly to Grandmother's specifications: wood floor, mirror, barre. The walls were painted wine red. Then Grandmother rejected the color as "hooker red" and had them painted birch green. In the end they were oxblood, which I could barely distinguish from hooker red. Grandfather had brought two workers with him to whom he talked in a language I didn't understand. They were small men who didn't look you in the eye. Their stained overalls flapped around their gaunt bodies.

"Who are these people?" I asked.

"Slaves," said my grandmother.

"That's a joke, right? He is paying them, isn't he?"

"I'm a woman, I don't have to know everything," said Grandmother.

I witnessed, for the first time, people taking orders from my grandfather. Up to now I'd only ever seen him at the bottom of the chain of command. At the top of our family pyramid was little Tschingis, sitting atop Grandmother's shoulders, of course. Now I saw with amazement that these men at least feared my grandfather. As soon as he opened his mouth they listened with intense looks on their faces and nodded eagerly.

"Do you beat them?" I asked during a break during which Grandmother brought by soljanka and plastic plates and tried in vain to suggest to the workers that they use wet wipes to clean their hands.

Grandfather looked at me from beneath his heavy eyelids. "You don't have to."

"Where did you find them?"

"I own a company."

"Does that mean you have even more people working for you?"

"I own a company."

"For how long?"

"The less you know, the easier you sleep," Grandmother interrupted. She put a piece of black bread into the unwashed hand of each worker. Ever since she'd been working on starting the ballet school, the girl from the photo—which for a while I'd kept safely under my pillow—flashed across her face time and time again. By this point I'd hidden it in a German-English dictionary and rarely pulled it out.

Grandmother smiled more, and it was no longer the grimace that used to make people cross the street. She no longer called Grandfather "old bag" or "Opa," and instead she said respectfully, "Father," and it made me feel as if I had been transported back to a time that I could never actually have witnessed.

"Look at him, look how Father gets the men to work," she said admiringly. And, "Father, I peeled you an apple for vitamins."

At the opening she was everything in one person: the owner, the director, the accountant, and the dance instructor. She let me write some text and take a photo of her at the barre. Vera and I went off after school to distribute flyers in the neighborhood postboxes. Amazingly, the number of registrations from Russian émigrés with little daughters skyrocketed even before the local paper ran virtually unaltered my text beneath the headline "Russian Ballet Star Brings Beauty to Troubled Neighborhood." Grandmother had the article framed and hung it on the wall of her tiny office.

That summer a young woman named Anastassia moved into the home; she was nothing but sinews and slender muscles and she applied to Grandmother's school with a formal resumé and certificates. My grandmother hired her as a dance instructor. From then on I liked to visit the school, which Grandmother took as a compliment, since she assumed that I missed her amidst all the confusion of my early onset puberty.

I drank tea from Grandmother's thermos and watched Anastassia through the two-way mirror, as Eastern European parents and grandparents dried their children's eyes and sent them back into the mirrored studio. The tea tasted and smelled particularly strong, and after I emptied the thermos I could no longer walk straight. Smoking a cigarette, Grandmother strolled out of the office during the lesson and into the changing room, where she nodded at parents.

"It's coming along," she said. Or: "I can't perform magic, you know." Sometimes also: "See my grandson over there? I nursed him back to health, willed him through his first years of life, fed him with a spoon, kept every speck of dust off him. And look at the way he carries himself. I should have sent him to ballet school. He's gay anyway."

On one of these afternoons, I was leaning over my homework in Grandmother's office, wedged between a desk, a coatrack, and an electric stove. Anastassia had nearly reached the end of her lessons, and was teaching the five-year-olds to bow elegantly. There was a knock, and a man entered and stood in front of Grandmother's desk.

"The owner isn't here," I said, trying to look past him into the studio. "Would you like to take a registration form? How old is your daughter?"

"I'm not here about my daughter," said the man.

I gestured with my pencil behind him. "Anastassia also has two boys in class. If any of the girls laugh at them, they get a smacking. Male honor is maintained here, after all every boy is a future defender of the Vaterland."

I didn't know myself why exactly I had quoted Anastassia word for word at that moment, maybe because she had smiled at me beforehand. I'd had too much of the tea, and my tongue felt unusually large and unwieldy. The man looked at me as if I was crazy.

"I'm Philipp," he said. His Russian sounded strange, as if he hadn't spoken it in years.

"I'm Max," I said.

"I know," he said.

I hiccupped and muttered that I needed fresh air. I staggered out of the office past him, leaned against a sycamore tree, and tried to breathe out Grandmother's tea, which seemed to have filled me from head to toe. The man followed me and stood next to me, visibly overwhelmed. When I swayed, he moved as if to catch me.

I looked at him and knew that he was the very man Grandmother had always warned me about. His shirt was ironed and was wet with sweat under the arms, which I could also feel running down my back, the day was unusually warm.

"Sir, are you the red-haired Jew?" my heavy tongue asked without checking with me first. I stared at his hair, which was streaked with silver strands.

"I used to be." He was putting great effort into not showing how much the sight of me disturbed him. "Is there someplace around here to get a coffee?"

I led him on shaky legs to the pedestrian zone, where two competing ice cream cafés had put chairs out on the sidewalk. I slumped with relief into a wicker chair at a small table. He sat down opposite me, his eyelid twitched, and the sight brought back a distant memory that I'd always thought was from a dream.

"It's nice here," said the man, and I nodded. The rest of this part of town consisted of apartment blocks and row houses, and the area had a bad reputation because of all the Russians. I leaned back and closed my eyes to try to slow the spinning.

"Would you like an ice cream?" asked the man.

I shook my head, which made me feel sicker.

"Have you been waiting for me?"

I shrugged.

"I found the dance school because of your grandmother's last name," he said. "She had threatened to have her husband kill me. She said he had a company."

I felt my lips forming a smile.

"I would be very grateful if you'd open your eyes."

I sighed. Even with my eyes open I could barely see anything, colorful mosquitos danced between me and the rest of the world, the man was blurry around the edges.

"What's your name anyway, sir?" I asked.

He dug around frantically in his chest pocket and put a

business card down on the table in front of me. "Philipp," he said, and I realized he'd already told me that. His twitching eyelid was driving me crazy.

"What is it you want, sir?" I asked.

"I don't know," he said. "Perhaps it would be nice if you addressed me less formally. What do you want?"

"Can you leave me a million?"

"What would you do with a million?"

I scratched my neck. "I'd buy my grandmother a house. She already has a dance school."

I enjoyed the look of horror on his face. Then I stood up and staggered off.

THE NUTCRACKER

I didn't tell anyone about it. Grandmother was so happy. She said so herself: "I'm so happy, Maxi. I don't know what I did to deserve it. Look at you, for instance. Nobody could tell what a failed mess you were just a few years ago. Imagine people meeting you in the street one day, people who didn't know you in the past, and having them think: the kid is totally normal. I never would have dared to dream that." Her left eye teared up with emotion.

Since I didn't know how to react to this, she continued: "My greatest joy is this wonder of a child. I've never experienced anything like it. I look at him and think, God has personally kissed me. I don't believe in God. But I never reckoned with the fact that he would bless me again with such a child." Now her right eye, too, was welling up, and she sniffled energetically and wiped her face.

"Look, Maxi. I have everything. I have children. I have a husband who respects me. He set up a dance school for me, and I have a chance to bestow on Germany a little beauty and taste. What more could I want?"

I didn't know, either.

"I even have a piano," said Grandmother triumphantly.

She had found it in a classified ad under the category "Free Stuff." The dark men in overalls had brought it in a van and carried it into the corner of the dance studio with their unwashed hands.

"What can one do? Animals," Grandmother said to me. "What do you think of the instrument, Maxi?"

I walked around it and touched it cautiously after I'd made sure my hands were clean. It was a strange light-yellow color, there was a piece of moth-eaten felt on the keys, and it was hopelessly out of tune. Nina said that, too, when Grandmother showed her the acquisition.

"Now we'll have live music for the Nutcracker," said Grandmother, who, thanks to her new status as piano owner, seemed to have grown a few centimeters taller.

"And who is supposed to play this thing?" asked Nina.

"Maxi here, of course."

I choked on my own spit. "Me? I can't."

"Why did you take lessons for all that time? And who was your teacher?" thundered Grandmother.

"He only had a broken-down keyboard to practice on. How was I supposed to do serious work with him?"

Grandmother sighed theatrically. "In that case old Margo will have to pay someone to play even though the family is full of musicians."

That year Grandmother experienced, as she put it, the most beautiful Christmas celebration of her life. "We have a child now and must be part of it," she said.

"And what was I the whole time—a poodle?" I asked.

She looked at me pityingly. "What is with you? The Germans are crazy about Christmas. You'll like it!"

My knowledge of German Christmas traditions had been supplied mostly by comics and television. Every year Christmas surprised me anew. In school I was out of my depth when the class did Secret Santa and everyone drew the name of a classmate from a hat to anonymously give gifts to. I never managed to stick to the specified price limit, and I put myself wholeheartedly into finding something adequate: a necklace or a nice bracelet that the recipient—I always drew a girl—would appreciate rather than laugh scornfully at every time. I'd never received anything other than soap or candles from my Secret Santa. Christmas flashed by me year after year without leaving a trace. I liked the peaceful days afterwards, though, when the shops were finally closed. In the kitchen were piles of cut-rate chocolate Santas that Grandmother had brought home and forbidden me to eat in the early years. I remembered suddenly how even then Grandfather had occasionally slipped me a piece.

I shared my—predominantly theoretical—knowledge with Grandmother. The stuff about the cookies she found foolish, but she had tried stollen once and while she didn't like it, she did respect it. The fact that so many Germans went to church at least on Christmas Eve surprised her disagreeably, and she asked with a trace of bad conscience whether there was a Christmas mass at the synagogue, where she hadn't shown up in ages.

She was, however, familiar with gift giving, from Russian New Year's celebrations. The tree for our celebration we usually got from the sidewalk shortly before New Year's Eve—if we were lucky it still had some tinsel on it—and we welcomed the new year with red beet salad and sparklers. I didn't know why we suddenly had to do everything differently now, but Grandmother seemed determined.

"Bring a tree home now, Father," she proclaimed at the beginning of December, wanting to do everything like the Germans this year. Nina contributed old Soviet tree decorations that were beautiful and fragile, like her. The Nutcracker rehearsals grew ever more intense, and there were the first cases of fainting in the studio and fistfights in the changing room, which made Grandmother proud: "We may be just a small outpost of the Russian ballet. But it's just like the real thing here."

The week before Christmas I heard Grandmother laughing upstairs at our door as I entered the staircase to our apartment building. A moment later the parcel deliveryman went past me panting and said he'd just left a Christmas gift for me with my darling mother.

Outside of the Secret Santa soap and candles, I'd never received a Christmas present, and I climbed the steps excitedly, two at a time.

"Did I get a package, Oma?"

I noticed in the hectic grimace that crossed her face for a moment that something wasn't right.

It might possibly have been due to my voice. Lately she'd kept telling me to speak more quietly, I was becoming a man too soon, and men's voices made her nervous. A shudder seemed to go through her, then she disappeared into the adjoining room and returned with the package.

I ripped it open and pulled out a dark blue ski jacket. From the sleeve fell the already familiar business card. I packed everything back into the box and pushed the package and its contents over to Grandmother.

"It's not a good color for you anyway," she said under her breath, and the panic in her voice made my heart flutter.

The Nutcracker performance on December 23rd was a total success. I'd never seen so many pretty girls at one time before. Anastassia was so radiant that Grandmother put her hand on her forehead. "You're glowing, dear girl, it must be scarlet fever."

Noise and light flickered in my head. The costumes were tasteful and restrained, but as for the room, Grandmother had been unable to contain herself: she probably bought up the town's entire tinsel stock. A grandiose twinkling Christmas tree blocked the entryway.

So as not to be petty, she gave a few of the flower bouquets that parents of the dancers handed her during extended calls of bravo to Anastassia and Nina. "I really must congratulate you: you barely made any mistakes, Nina."

Grandfather, who'd sat next to me during the performance, stashed the leftover flowers, wine, and gift baskets in the car. I suspected he had fallen asleep during the show. Though maybe he had just listened with his eyes closed. But then little Tschingis got restless on my lap, and Grandfather had sat up with a start and taken him outside.

"What did you think of the premiere, Father?" asked Grandmother before Grandfather squeezed into the car among the gift baskets.

"It was lovely. But nobody danced better than you, Rita."

"And what did you think, my little treasure?"

"I was blown away."

"Nina played nicely, too, don't you think?" Grandmother was generous in her moment of joy.

"Yeah, the music was very nice."

At this point Vera cleared her throat. I waited for her to stop on her own, but eventually I hit her between the shoulder blades with all my strength, and she finally fell silent. Among all the red-cheeked glitter-girls she looked small and unimpressive in her brown sweater, and I could have sworn that she knew it.

Anastassia was standing next to us. It looked as if she would like to have come home with us to celebrate the premiere and the impending Christmas holiday. But Grandmother patted her on the cheek.

"I'm sorry, dear child. Find yourself an invitation somewhere else. It's just for closest family, you understand?"

"Sounds like a funeral," muttered Nina.

FATHER FROST

On Christmas Eve I was awakened by Grandmother frantically and loudly crinkling the chocolate out of the advent calendar that was sitting in front of her on the table.

"Who is that from?" I asked.

"From me. Who else would give you something?"

"It's for me?"

"Who else? How many grandchildren do I have? But I forgot it in the cabinet." She shoved the last piece of chocolate into her mouth. "Don't bother me. I need to concentrate."

It could almost have been a real Christmas, but then she pushed things too far. We sat down to eat far too early—supposedly because little Tschingis was getting impatient. In reality it was Grandmother who couldn't stand waiting any longer. After everyone had poked around in the Russian herring appetizer from the nearby supermarket, she got up secretively and left the room. Vera and I exchanged glances. Nina arranged red beets on a plate, not paying attention. Grandfather rocked little Tschingis on his knee.

I had a creeping dread about what was coming, but hoped that I was wrong. I gave up hope when a violent rumble shook the hallway. Through the doorway, which suddenly seemed too narrow, came a fat figure in a red coat. It had on heavy boots and a conspicuous pillow that was supposed to pass for a fat belly. A red pointy hat was pulled down over the eyebrows, but the worst of all was the matted gray beard.

"Are there any good children here?" bellowed the figure. Vera cringed. The eyes of the figure, hopelessly familiar and strange at the same time, glanced at me and begged for support.

"Here," I croaked.

"Can you recite a poem for Ded Moroz?"

Grandfather looked up from his plate. Nina was speechless. Vera giggled into my shoulder. I shoved her away and stood up. I had to play along so that Grandmother could save face. But at that moment a deafening scream rose, one that sounded more like a siren than a human voice.

"No, don't!" Grandmother ripped down the beard and fell to her knees in front of little Tschingis. "It's just me, your Margo! Don't you recognize me?"

Tschingis turned away, burying his face in my grandfather's chest and pushing away Grandmother's hands.

"The costume is too good! He believed it, my little sparrow!" Grandmother was near tears herself. She quickly took off the coat, trying to show it to Tschingis, but he didn't want to look and just quietly whimpered.

"It's me! Don't cry! Ded Moroz brought you many gifts. Look, socks. Mittens. The watch is for Father, but he'll let you play with it. Just look now, don't cry. This bottle here, this is for your mother. Don't try to tell me that anyone has ever given you anything like this before, Nina. This is Chanel No. 5, I would have killed for it at your age. Though you're not so young anymore. A calculator for Maxi and a dictionary so he won't make so many mistakes. Shower gel for the girl Vera, never hurts. Why are you crying, my little treasure? Tschingis! Maya! I was just having a bit of fun!"

THE MOVE

I had long since figured out that it was a law of nature: Grandmother and Nina couldn't both be doing well at the same time. Grandmother was completely convinced that she had become a successful entrepreneur and artist and had pulled off a fantastic Christmas for her family. She talked about it for months afterwards. So, naturally, I asked Vera how Nina was doing and my fears were confirmed.

"Today she talked about France," said Vera. "She read recently that Russian musicians are still valued there. But it was in a book that was pretty old."

"What does she want to do in France?" I asked.

"No idea," said Vera, shrugging. A few days later she gave me the latest: "Canada. She saw a postcard. The nature is breathtaking."

"It's cold in Canada. She gets cold so easily."

"I'll tell her," promised Vera and reported back at the next chance. "No, it's the US. She says it's a land of limitless opportunities."

We usually lay in my grandfather's cot, as I thought it inappropriate to invite a girl onto our shared couch in Grandmother's absence. Once she found a strand of Vera's light-brown hair on it and broke out in tears. I'd stood next to her and helplessly patted her shoulder.

"Leave Oma, Maxi," she'd murmured. "You've gotten so big, I can't understand a word of what you say anymore. Sometimes I think you can't speak Russian anymore."

"I don't believe you're going to leave," I said to Vera.

"Shut your mouth. You haven't even managed to move out of the home." She looked at me for a long time; I met her gaze until she looked away, disappointed.

In June, on the way home from school Vera said we wouldn't be in the same class anymore. Nina had found a job and an apartment somewhere else. It wasn't France and not even Berlin, but the nearest big city, which you could get to in forty minutes on the regional train. I answered: "That's a lot closer than Canada, too bad for you!" and I was surprised at Vera's hurt expression.

At home, Grandmother was sitting on the couch crying. I knelt down in front of her and took her hand. Her back, which was always so straight, was hunched. Her hair hung down, stringy. The powder on her face was clotted and allowed red splotches on her cheeks to show. She must have been sitting there a long time, and though she slowly managed to stop the flow of tears, she couldn't stop sobbing.

"Who died?" I asked. She had told me frequently of late that this or that great aunt was no longer among the living. Since I'd spent many years under the impression that I had no family beyond my grandparents, it was difficult for me to feign much sorrow. Grandmother didn't go to any of the funerals since her Russian passport had expired years ago.

"Nina," she rasped, taking her hand away from me. "Nina is leaving."

"Is that really so bad?" I asked.

The short pause had allowed my grandmother to replenish her supply of tears and they began to flow again.

"Is Opa going with her?" I asked.

She looked at me as if I were crazy.

"She wants to take Tschingis with her," she whispered. "She doesn't have any idea what he needs. How will the child get by without me?"

"You don't see him so often anymore. You're so busy."

"I'm always there when he needs me. She doesn't have any family there. Everything she has is here in this backwater."

I silently stroked her arm. Since she'd been running the dance school she'd lost weight, her arms were bony, the first age spots covered with a makeup pencil. Her nails were cut short and unpolished. Suddenly she wrapped both hands around my head and pulled me to her chest so that I could hear her fast, sometimes stuttering heartbeat.

"Everyone is leaving. Only Maxi stays with me," she said. "Promise? At least you still need Oma, right?"

"Of course," I said, trying desperately to breathe in her embrace.

Nina looked elated as she packed her books and sheet music into moving boxes. In the middle of the room stood a giant pile where she threw scarves, gloves, and random plastic bags. Tschingis sat in the corner and played with a pack of matches. I greeted the two of them and went quickly into Vera's room.

"At least admit that you're sad, too," Vera murmured after I'd assembled a few of the moving boxes my grandfather had brought to the apartment in stacks.

"I'm sad."

"I don't believe you. You're happy to be rid of me. You get this apartment, and you'll finally have your own room and then, no doubt, soon a girlfriend."

I smiled at the fact that she had such thoughts.

She threw a rolled-up pair of socks at me. I caught it and sat down on the floor cross-legged.

"What goes in first? Underwear?"

She shrugged and stayed sitting on the bed.

"I don't know," she said.

It made me think of how Grandmother normally packed

her suitcase. She'd open it on the bed, which she had already covered with foil because naturally suitcases were contaminated with germs. Then she'd throw things into it, haphazardly and with no organization, clean and dirty laundry, swimsuits and wool socks, unopened medicine packages, dried herbs, old maps that had nothing to do with where she was going, slippers, always slippers, little Orthodox travel icons, dish towels, disinfected cutlery. Then she would try to close the suitcase with the aid of brawn and my body weight.

When it didn't work, she'd dump the contents out in the middle of the room and bemoan the fact that because of her wretched living conditions she was unable to deal with getting things together to travel, until my grandfather would push the pile aside with his foot and quickly and systematically fill the suitcase with the necessary items—though he forgot the toothbrush every single time. It had been the same when we went to Spain. Following that trip, Grandmother had managed to wriggle out of the contract obligating her to take an annual trip to Spain for the rest of her life. It hadn't occurred to her to look at the fine print before signing it. Though she wouldn't have understood anyway.

I opened Vera's drawer and tried to do what my grandfather would have done in this situation. I transferred the manageable contents into the moving boxes, making sure that no heavy items went on top of breakables, that all smaller items were stowed in bags or smaller boxes. Now and again I picked up a sock with a hole in it or an old school notebook. Vera shrugged as if none of it had anything to do with her, and tossed the item in a garbage bag.

At some point my grandparents joined in. Grandmother sat with Tschingis in the corner, took away the matches, kissed him and tried to get him interested in a memory game, while my grandfather and I carried garbage bags down. A little van was waiting in front of the door, and two wiry men carried down the boxes and few pieces of furniture in the tiniest amount of time. The van drove off.

Nina and Vera followed Grandfather outside and got into his light-blue VW. Grandmother carried Tschingis down and ordered me to strap him into his child seat, so many children died because of failure to follow the instructions and it would really be a shame in his case. After that she pressed a cooler bag filled with sandwiches into Nina's hands. Finally she turned to Vera: "Be respectable. You see what can happen otherwise."

Vera nodded.

"Drive carefully, Father," said Grandmother, and something in her voice made me prick up my ears. At the same time I knew that I had better not look her in the face, so I focused on the passenger door, on the other side of which Nina was unfolding a map. "Drive gently. This isn't construction debris you're transporting, Father," Grandmother continued, but Grandfather didn't seem to hear her. He drove off without turning to look at us.

We stood next to each other, the key to Nina's apartment in hand, until we could no longer see the taillights. Only then did we stop waving.

"He's not coming back," said Grandmother. "Now it's just you and me. Too bad that the Jewish girl is gone. Would have been good for you because she's got such a crush on you that she could eat you up. And ugly enough that nobody would steal her from you."

WILLY WONKA

Grandfather returned after two nights. He put down the car keys on the wobbly cabinet in the entryway that Grandmother had found left out with the garbage and then filled with her own garbage.

Grandfather went silently into the bathroom in order to wash his hands thoroughly even though Tschingis wasn't there. Grandmother followed him and watched him soap his fingers.

"Are you hungry, Father?"

He nodded.

"Of course. But I haven't made anything."

He shrugged his shoulders.

"Did you set out hungry? Did she not pack you anything for the ride?"

He turned his severe gaze toward her, and she went silent and walked into the kitchen to put on water to boil.

She was too proud to ask him for details. In order to spare her the humiliation, I asked questions in her place even though I wasn't particularly interested in the answers: What did Nina's new apartment look like? Did Tschingis really have his own room? What did a little child need his own room for? Had he cried during the trip? How far away was Nina's new music school? How many bandits were there drifting around the streets of the big city? Could you see anything through all the smog? Did they already have a telephone? The questions shot out of me and Grandfather answered them with a nod, a shake of the head, or a shrug until I was no longer sure anymore which reaction went with which question. Grandmother followed our conversation attentively.

Not a week had gone by before Grandmother called Nina. Their conversation lasted just a few sentences, then Nina gave the phone to little Tschingis. I noticed the change in Grandmother's voice, which immediately shot up, tender and high-pitched. Grandmother asked what Tschingis was eating and what he was dreaming about. She told him that she now lived in his apartment and that I, his nephew, had moved into Vera's room. Grandmother had taken over the living room, and Grandfather was sleeping on the cot in the kitchen, which was folded up each morning and set aside. I had barely noticed the move: more men from Grandfather's company had packed up our scant belongings in no time at all, driven to Nina's, and unloaded everything again.

"Are you Willy Wonka?" I had asked Grandfather.

He had nodded as if he knew what I was talking about.

I went into Vera's room and lay down on the bed that had belonged to her. Grandmother had changed the sheets and disinfected the bedframe, but I still caught the scent of Vera's hair. From the bed I could see the acacia tree in front of the window. I found it strange that I missed Vera so little.

The move into Nina's apartment seemed to have sealed for Grandmother the tragic nature of emigration once and for all.

"Now we're stuck here," she said, walking from one window to the next and casting frustrated glances into the interior courtyard, at the barren patch of lawn, the laundry lines, and the rusty Ping-Pong table. "All because of you Jews."

I didn't point out to her that she'd been stuck here for years already and that she'd been the one who'd initiated the whole exodus in the first place. No other family had held out as long as we had in the refugee home. The atmosphere had changed over the years: the more recent refugees didn't speak Russian and filled the common hallways with loads of family members and disorganized piles of stuff. Grandmother had used her nail scissors to puncture more than one ball that had rolled to her feet and taken more than one bicycle that she'd stumbled over to the police.

"I actually preferred the Jews," she'd hissed, kicking boxes of donated clothing and diapers out of her way. "At least they don't spawn like rabbits and speak a normal language. We need to get out of here, Maxi, or else we'll wake up one day with our throats cut. Only your grandfather will be spared, the old slit-eye. But what would he do without old Margo?"

Nina's apartment, our new home, was on the top floor of a five-story gray residential building. It was filled with mus-tached German married couples and hard-working Turkish families, who lived alongside each other peacefully. They took turns cleaning the staircase, but not Grandmother, who found the system unhygienic and the cleaning plan an imposition.

Since the move she'd lost interest in the dance school, and I worried that the next Nutcracker performance could fall through if the ever-thinner Anastassia had to handle everything on her own. I still liked to do my homework in Grandmother's office, but I drank cola instead of her tea. During breaks Anastassia came in with an energy drink, sat down on my schoolwork, and insisted I massage her feet.

Instead of taking care of the new student contracts, Grandmother mostly sat on a bench in front of our new home and chatted about life with another grandmother who wore a scarf on her head and was small and round and likewise spoke no German. A thermos sat between the two of them, and Grandmother had brought two cups. Her braid hung down heavily, disheveled, and I had a mean suspicion that she no longer made the effort to redo it each morning. I thought it was long overdue that she dye the roots again, but Grandmother just waved her hand dismissively when I offered my help. She sat there slumped, and the sight made me get a lump in my throat. I only understood what good posture was after Grandmother gave up on it.

When she tossed out a "you miss her, Father, eh?" to my Grandfather when he came home, he and I exchanged worried looks. Grandfather began to take evening strolls with Grandmother, even though she initially protested against it bitterly: "Am I some kind of circus horse that has to always walk in circles?" After Grandmother instructed me not to touch her cigarettes and not to set the apartment on fire as if I were six years old, I watched out the window as they walked around the block side by side.

Sometimes they went farther, and I couldn't even see them from the balcony. They often came back from longer walks with ice cream cones which they'd eaten all the way down to the end.

Once they had a pizza box upon their return. "Father wanted to indulge old Margo," said Grandmother, licking strings of cheese from her fingers. "It's Italian, Maxi. It's called P-I-Z-Z-A. They know a thing or two, the Italians. I would never have believed it."

The following week, we got take-out pizza every night, until Grandmother said: "Father, I'm making you poor," and he caressed her wrist, making her blush. Another day they went together to the movie theater around the corner, though they had to leave the show early and Grandmother came home with red, crying eyes. There'd been a small child in the film the same age as Tschingis.

Fall came and I began to worry about the coming Christmas celebrations. Grandfather still sat on the balcony despite the cold weather, blowing smoke into the still blossoming snapdragons he had planted for Grandmother. I stood there and wondered when I'd be old enough to start smoking, too, when he held up his finger. A bird had started singing in the distance.

"Go get Nina," Grandfather said to me.

I was sure he'd misspoken. I slowly turned to him to give him a chance to correct his mistake. He looked at me intently as if waiting for something, then looked at the open balcony door and called inside: "Nina dear! Come out here!"

Something clanged deep inside the apartment. Then Grandmother popped out, wiping her hands on her apron, her mouth already open, but the curses lodged in her throat. My grandfather stretched out his hand to her, and as she neared him and put her hand in his, he pulled her onto his lap.

I turned away, pushed past the two of them, and went into my room.

MIDDLE C

Grandmother had arranged for the piano from the dance studio to be transported home and made Anastassia use a tape player instead. The piano would need to be retuned again. In our apartment it seemed big and miserable like a dog tied up at a highway rest stop.

"The woman has no conscience," said my grandmother. "I would never just leave a piano behind. She knows that nobody will play it since she drove the music out of Maxi."

If I came home from school and quietly opened the door with my own key—Vera had secretly given me hers, because I'd never have gotten my own from Grandmother—sometimes I would hear her talking aloud: "Sitting there all alone, you poor thing. But Margo will take care. She'll dust you off nicely, then we'll get a tuner. It doesn't matter that you're old. You're not a woman, for you a few years don't matter as long as everything inside is in order." She knocked gently on the wood with a dirty laugh.

When I entered the room she pulled her hand back and hid it behind her back. "Can't you see? I'm dusting." To prove it she held up one of Grandfather's old ribbed undershirts. "Do you think you can clean the keys with dishwashing detergent?"

"No idea," I said.

Once I came home and heard from the staircase that someone was fooling around on the keys. I sat on the steps and listened, smiling. Sometimes I recognized a couple notes and realized Grandmother was trying to play one of the

German children's songs from my old beginner's music book. I waited until the piano fell silent and only then went inside the apartment.

When, later that same night, I took down the garbage, I found Grandfather on the staircase. He was standing a floor below ours and alternately staring at one of the doors, where a dried wreath hung, and the key ring in his hand. I took him by the hand and wanted to go upstairs with him, but he balked and gestured toward an open window facing the courtyard. Now I, too, heard the melody wafting into our staircase, having made its labyrinthine way from some other apartment. It was the song "Greek Wine," and Grandfather seesawed in rhythm to it. His eyes glistened. I wanted to ask him whether he liked the song, but then I felt as if it would be intrusive. We stood silently next to each other until the song ended.

Afterwards we went upstairs together. He sat in the chair in the entryway for a long time before taking off his shoes. It didn't escape Grandmother's notice that he reacted to the sound of her voice with a cringe. She immediately went quiet and served him his dinner silently.

I showed Grandmother where middle C was and how she could count out all the other notes from there. She was impressed: "It wasn't all for nothing, the expensive lessons!" Ever since I'd sat on the staircase most afternoons, smoking or reading, while Grandmother practiced simple melodies. I knew that she'd jump up immediately as soon as she heard me, as if she didn't want to be caught in the middle of an obscene act.

Once I fell asleep and only woke up when the cigarette I'd been smoking fell and burned a hole in my sneaker. I stomped it out, put the still-hot butt in the cup of my hand, which I hid behind my back, and went into the apartment. Grandmother's voice came loud and excited from the kitchen.

"Have you no conscience? Being together with a man is more than whoring. It's a duty, like with a child. It means making soup and ironing socks. You're chained to him forever, and if he needs you, you can't moan that the wife is always responsible for everything."

I leaned against the wall and held my breath. The palm of my hand burned. Next to my head was a framed picture of a rural winter landscape that Nina had left behind.

"That's the way upstanding people are," said my grandmother. "It's not a question of having fun, this isn't a brothel."

Once she'd been silent for a while, I slammed the apartment door demonstratively and stuck my head into the kitchen. "Who were you on the phone with?"

"Nobody," said Grandmother irritated.

"But I heard your voice."

"I wasn't on the phone!" she shouted. "When will you stop snooping around behind my back? The soup's on the stove!"

That night I was awoken by an unfamiliar noise. It sounded as if at least a dozen feet were tromping past my door, and a babble of voices filled the air. I filtered a few words out, which were vaguely reminiscent of Russian.

I jumped up and ran out of my room, past strange men in stained overalls who stepped aside respectfully. Grandfather was sitting in the kitchen, a trail of blood had followed along behind him. His right hand was oddly twisted, siting on the kitchen table, and Grandmother was pouring water over it. Grandfather smiled as if it all had nothing to do with him. Blood flowed down his face from a large wound on his forehead.

"What happened?" I whispered, and Grandmother yelled: "What is the child doing in the kitchen?"

"Psst, little one," said my grandfather, stretching out his uninjured hand. "Come here, Maya my treasure, your mother doesn't mean any harm. The loudest dogs don't bite."

I took a step back. Grandmother froze. "Father, this is Maxi. Maya's son. Your children look like they all came off the same conveyor belt. No wonder you mix them up."

"Tschingis Tschingisovich was up on the scaffolding," said one of the mustachioed men standing at the very front of the group. "I'm sorry, madam, nobody expected this."

"That's how it always is," said Grandmother. "None of you expect anything. What's wrong, Father? Stop! Stop it immediately!" She let out a piercing scream. At first I thought she was upset about the bloodstain on her nightgown. Then I realized that she was propping up my slumping grandfather with her entire body.

General Diet Meal

"Why did you bring the child with you?" hissed my grandmother.

"Where should I have left him?"

"There are germs in the hospital, if he touches anything here he'll be contaminated down to his bones!"

"Was I supposed to leave him alone? Or with his not exactly helpful sister? I don't have anybody else."

"Is that my fault?!"

"What do you want from me, Margarita Ivanovna?"

I listened and watched Nina and Grandmother through half-closed eyes, pushed into the chair by the weight of Tschingis, who had fallen asleep on the way and had been handed to me immediately upon arrival. Grandfather lay in the hospital bed with his head wrapped in bandages, smiling. His eyes were closed, I wasn't sure whether he was awake the entire time, listening and finding it amusing, or whether he was dreaming of something particularly nice.

Nina and Grandmother leaned over the bed from opposite sides. Grandmother fussed worriedly over him the whole time, adjusting the pillows, the sheets, even the bandages. Nina held back, sometimes she winced as if trying to choke back tears. Her motions seemed harder and older. She hadn't hugged me when greeting me, instead she'd briefly patted my arm as if I, too, might have something to do with the share of misfortune she'd managed to foist back in my grandmother's direction.

"Nothing is sacred to you young women anymore," said Grandmother bitterly. "Though you're not so young anymore, either, Nina!"

Grandfather opened his eyes, his smile broadened. A gorgeous dark-skinned nurse brought in food on a tray. Grandmother lifted the plastic cover and eyed the gray slice of bread, sausage, and slice of pickle alongside a container of vanilla pudding laid out on the tray.

"What is this?" she asked, and the feigned calmness in her voice portended a storm on the horizon.

"General diet meal."

"Send this muck back to Africa." Grandmother shoved the tray away. She still spoke half in Russian.

"Give it to me," said Nina. The nurse retreated after giving me a pitying smile, and Grandmother shook her head.

Nina chewed with purposeful indifference while Grandmother retrieved the pot-bellied glass jars in which she'd transported chicken soup and steamed broccoli. Grandfather let a few spoonfuls pass his lips. Nina glanced over at me.

"What's new?"

"Nothing," I said. "You?"

She shrugged. I ran my hand over Tschingis's sweaty tuft of hair. "He's gotten bigger. Has he got a rash on his face?"

"Probably dirt," said Grandmother. "Or he ate something bad. Maxi would have been a wreck if he'd been brought up in the big city, I can tell you, Nina. That's why I was happy we landed in this backwater. Nothing happening at all, you could kill yourself out of boredom, not even a river nearby, but at least there are no felonies committed in broad daylight. I've never opted for fun, but always opted instead to meet my responsibilities. We all declared ourselves Jews for the sake of the poor child, do you understand what kind of sacrifice that is, Nina? Nothing personal. Tschingis on the other hand is an extraordinary boy, never seen such an intelligent gaze. A bit like Maya. Give him to me to raise, Nina, I'll make an American president out of him."

"It's plenty for you to support him with phone calls," said Nina. "I can always cook noodles while you're talking to him."

"You know, of course, that noodles are nothing but flour, which clogs the digestive system. I always prepared fresh vegetables for my grandchild."

"If I had a medal, I'd pin it on you."

I made sure Tschingis didn't slip out of my lap. I didn't want him to be woken up because Grandmother and Nina, though still speaking in indoor voices, were talking more loudly now. Grandfather reached for the hands of the two women, who were still leaning on either side of the bed. He found them and caressed them simultaneously. "Psst, Maya," he said. "Why so sad? Your mother loves you more than anything in the world."

Nina gasped. "Maya?"

"You'll never be able to compete with Maya, madam," said Grandmother. "You'll never overtake her, no matter how much piano you play."

Tschingis stretched in my lap. He slid down from my lap and I made sure he landed softly on the floor. He paused for a few seconds kneeling between my legs and bracing himself on my thighs with his elbows. He stared at me. He had Grandfather's eyes, the same severity and calm.

"Do you still recognize me?" I whispered, and he smiled.

He fell asleep immediately on the air mattress that had been set up in my room; he was a good sleeper. Me, on the other hand, I lay awake the whole time and listened to the voices in the kitchen. Grandmother was holding forth about the duties that came with being a woman. While she got quieter over the course of the evening, the urgency of Nina's voice rose.

"Make less money than a cleaning woman," I heard. "The

monthly public transport pass eats up a fortune . . . Of course I blame myself . . . Therapy . . . alone with no family in the big city . . . doesn't want to go to daycare. Cries."

"Daycare is for children nobody wants," said Grandmother, throwing grease on the fire.

"What's left of my life . . ."

"You'll be dead and buried one day, who'll ask about your life then?"

"Vera despises me."

"Tell me about it. I've done everything on my own for my entire life. Totally gray by the age of thirty. Every year counts triple for me."

"Double," I muttered under my breath. Tschingis turned over and sighed in his sleep.

Before getting ready for school the next morning, I cleaned up the bottles and empty glasses. Several coffee cups were filled with cigarette butts. I cast a glance into the living room, where Grandmother and Nina were sharing the couch, then I closed the door quietly.

From a phone booth I called the number at Nina's new apartment. A man answered and I asked him to put Vera on the phone. I had to wait a suspiciously long time; there was cursing in the background.

"What do you want?" asked Vera hoarsely when she finally came to the phone. I told her that her mother and her brother had arrived safely and that I would look out for them.

"As if I wanted to know that," said Vera and hung up.

The dismissal of my grandfather from the hospital couldn't come quickly enough for Grandmother. She was afraid that the doctors would realize he wasn't all there anymore. When they examined him or changed his bandages, she always tried to distract them whenever they directed any questions at Grandfather. Of course, she misunderstood most of what they said and talked in Russian to the medical staff. The nurses began to avoid Grandfather's room.

Despite Grandmother's fears, nobody tried to keep Grandfather in the hospital or commit him to a psychiatric ward. When I went to the hospital the nurses called me into their conference room and gave me cola and gummi bears and asked who the two women at Grandfather's bedside were and which of them had adopted me and my cute little brother from Korea.

On the day Grandfather was released, Grandmother frantically packed his bag, tied his shoes, and accompanied him with Nina's help to the parking lot and into his old VW, which one of Grandfather's workers had driven there and left for us.

Grandfather sat at the steering wheel and waited patiently. Grandmother looked questioningly at Nina. Nina shrugged.

"How are you feeling, Father?" asked Grandmother unnecessarily loudly.

"Very well."

"Do you think you are able to drive a car?"

"Of course.

"And you know who I am, right?"

"Margarita Ivanovna, I beg you!" whispered Nina reproachfully.

"Don't tell him!" hissed Grandmother. "Do you at least know who this is here?" She gestured to Nina. Grandmother's mood visibly changed at my grandfather's sheepish grin. "And this person?" She pointed at me.

"My beloved grandchild."

"And who is Maya?"

"I let her down," said Grandfather under his breath.

"All clear. He's fine today," said Grandmother matter-of-factly and got into the passenger seat as I opened the back door for Nina.

SOMEWHERE IN THERE IS A HUMAN SOUL

Nina made many attempts to extricate herself from us. The first time Grandmother cursed her for seven generations, with the exception of little Tschingis and his offspring. The second time Grandmother just waved it aside: "I know that somewhere in there is a human soul. They'll be back here soon." On Nina's third attempt to flee Grandmother just shrugged her shoulders. "Do whatever you want, Nina. I'm not your lover, chasing after you constantly." That time Nina made it as far as the train station.

Grandmother was convinced that Grandfather couldn't be left out of sight for a second, or else something would happen to him—he could walk in front of a car, get beat up, or climb over the railing of a bridge. Unsupervised, he was in greater danger than little Tschingis, she imagined. In principle, she said, little Tschingis could even look after the big one in an emergency, if for no other reason than pure mental capacity. In the end, it boiled down to one normal person—Grandmother herself, Nina, and to a somewhat lesser extent me—having to be at Grandfather's side around the clock with little Tschingis in tow.

Grandfather left the apartment only to check to make sure things were going alright at the construction sites once in a while. He accepted his new chaperones placidly. I was sure that he was clearheaded and went along with the whole charade just to keep Grandmother busy and Nina placated. When I asked him if I could turn on the radio when we were driving, he said: "Ask Tschingis."

The workers, too, got used to the new arrangement. They stopped taking off their paint-smeared baseball caps and went ahead and finished their smelly hand-rolled cigarettes when either of the alternating women appeared. In one corner, on a plastic tarp, waited an upturned bucket covered with an embroidered cushion. Sometimes there was a beer or dark-black coffee from a thermos for the madam, for little Tschingis pats on the head and gifts. The men seemed ageless, but I knew from Grandfather that nearly all of them had left large families back home. They looked at my little uncle with a mix of heartache and tenderness. One of them spent nights making him toys out of matchboxes and gave Tschingis piece by piece a train with many carriages, a street with skyscrapers, and pieces of furniture for a dollhouse.

When both Grandmother and Nina were unable to do it and I had Grandfather duty, I sat on the embroidered cushion and watched as with barely a word Grandfather made sure walls were torn down and new wires were installed. If I had to wait too long, out of boredom I sketched strange things I saw at the construction sites: newspapers I couldn't understand even though they were in Cyrillic letters, tin cans that seemed to have come straight out of a black-and-white film, well-worn glossy magazines full of celebrities completely unknown to me, porn magazines that had been quickly stashed away from me but that I found anyway, homemade camping stoves, and a fish hung out to dry, which stank beyond belief. I helped myself from Grandmother's wallet to buy stamps and sent the sketches to Vera. Although she never answered me, I was sure that she eagerly went to the mailbox every day.

Nina's appearance brought Grandmother, as she was so fond of saying, a spark of relief and a bonfire of problems. The biggest of them she would never have admitted even under torture: in Nina's presence she didn't trust herself to play piano.

It was the first time I ever experienced my grandmother feeling embarrassed. Sometimes she tried to send Nina out with Grandfather: "You need to take Father out for some fresh air!"

"I didn't know that Tschingis Tschingisovich needed to be taken out for a walk like a dog."

"Everybody needs to breathe!"

"What do you think he's doing all the time?" asked Nina, and my grandfather called from the balcony, where he was watching the crows in the treetops: "I promise you, Rita dear, I am breathing just fine!"

But it wasn't more than fifteen minutes before Nina threw on her jacket and helped my grandfather into his shoes. I had missed the moment at which they started to treat him not only as if he were crazy but also as if he were infirm. I couldn't discern any change in him. While everything else was in flux, Tschingis getting bigger, Grandmother getting smaller, and Nina getting plumper, Grandfather always stayed the same. Nina linked arms with him, and I saw how much effort it took Grandmother not to yell, "Stop whoring around!" after them, even though she had just personally escorted the two of them out of the apartment.

"Are they gone?" she asked, recklessly leaning over the railing of the balcony. "And Maxi, wouldn't you like to get some air as well?"

"Why?" I asked, sitting on the bed immersed in Stephen King's *It*.

"To play. Other boys your age go out all the time and play. Perhaps there might also be a girl on the street who won't run away from you?"

I took pity on her, grabbed my book, and left the apartment. I could have gone to see Anastassia at the dance school, but usually I sat on the staircase and read, leaning against the wall as the sound of awkward playing pressed into my ears. Grandmother had worked her way through the children's piano book with the balloons on the cover, and I had secretly bought her one called *For the Adult Piano Student* and stashed it under her old medical textbooks. I could be sure that she wouldn't know whether she might have bought it herself somewhere along the line.

Grandmother couldn't decide whether she detested big or small cities more. She hated the place that had become our home, and since Nina's move she no longer made any secret of it. I had internalized the idea that it was because of me that she had buried herself alive in the middle of nowhere, while other women dragged their families into the dangers of a metropolis on a whim. Grandmother knew a lot about big cities, and our emigration wasn't only about fleeing the future, but also about escaping car exhaust and criminality, even though she herself absolutely knew the joys of an inspiring metropolis. The first year in Germany I totally believed that I wouldn't have managed to stay alive for two minutes in Frankfurt.

I was ashamed by the sense of triumph I felt when I got out at the main train station.

Vera was standing on the platform, small and pale among the commuters scurrying about, and she didn't see me until I was right in front of her. "Don't grin so idiotically," she said, grabbing my hand with her hot, rough fingers and pulling me along behind her until we reached a side street.

"Where should we go?" I asked. "Where do you guys live?"

"Are you nuts? We can't go to our place."

"Why not?"

"Too far," said Vera, and I knew she was lying.

I stuck my hand in my jacket pocket and felt for the money I had stolen from Grandmother's wallet. Then I opened the door of a small café. Maybe Grandmother had been right, and I would never become a man. But there was one thing I could do.

"What do you want to eat?" I asked.

We didn't manage to tell each other anything. Vera gulped down two pieces of cake and a sandwich, drank two cups of hot chocolate, and demanded again, this time with a full mouth, that I stop grinning so idiotically. She didn't ask about her mother, and even less about my grandparents. I tried to tell her about them, but she held her hot hand in front of my mouth. I briefly grazed her hand with my lips and asked whether there was anyone taking care of her now that she no longer had me. She mumbled: "If you only knew."

She took me back to the platform. When the regional train entered the station, I took Vera's hand. "My father also lives somewhere around here," I said. "I have his address."

"What?" Vera shouted. "You only tell me that now? Where exactly does he live?"

I boarded the train with the feeling that I had missed out on something important.

The first time I awoke with a start because I'd heard tentative footsteps in the apartment, I rolled over and quickly fell asleep again with the hope that somebody else would look into it. The second time, it was clear that nobody except me was hearing it. I got up, carefully climbed over sleeping Tschingis on the air mattress, and looked around for the source of the noise. Grandmother was sleeping with whistling breaths next to Nina on the couch, a sight that immediately chased me from the room. I still hadn't gotten used to it.

The apartment door was ajar, and when I stepped barefoot onto the staircase, I discovered Grandfather on the stairs that led up. Above us was only the roof.

When Grandfather saw me, he smiled sheepishly. I acted as if it was the most normal thing in the world to meet him on the staircase in the middle of the night with toes contorted by the cold. I took his hand and led him back into the apartment, where I locked the door and secured it with the chain. When I saw him sitting at the kitchen table the next morning freshly shaved and dressed, the memory of the night before seemed like a dream, and I couldn't make up my mind whether to tell Nina or Grandmother about it.

For months now, Grandfather had behaved unremarkably during the day. Once in a while I saw him out on the balcony staring into the sky.

Grandmother interpreted his behavior her own way. One morning she took the tram to a gourmet food shop and brought home figs, pomegranates, and stuffed grape leaves. She presented the purchases proudly to Grandfather. He smiled politely and turned away.

"Didn't touch a thing," Grandmother complained to Nina that evening. "I should have known. Back in the village they had figs as sweet as honey, pomegranates as big as a child's head. The fruit here is a pale imitation. Since we've been in this country he's not touched a single bite of melon."

"The stuff's really not that bad." Nina helped herself to some of the grape leaves.

"You don't have any sense of taste."

"Is he homesick?"

"What kind of question is that. Who among us isn't homesick? You don't have to beat a dead horse."

"He never talked much to me."

"Maybe he's become deaf and dumb over the years?" Grandmother speculated aloud. "You know what, Nina, you should go back to your filthy crime-infested city. Do you think I don't know you have a lover waiting in your apartment? You're just incapable of making up your mind, that's your problem. You're fickle. When I was younger, I was the same way. But the fun of that will pass when you eventually get to be as old as I am."

"I don't know if I'll make it that long," said Nina. "In your company every year counts for two, or what was it again?"

It was lucky for her that she ended up staying for a few more nights anyway. She'd certainly never have forgiven herself for it is she hadn't.

I regretted having revealed my father's address to Vera. She called me and told me about the building he lived in.

"It's giant," she whispered into the phone while Grandmother talked in my other ear because she thought I was discussing my homework with a classmate.

"The fence is so high. I think there's a pool behind the building, but I'm not sure. Should I have rung the doorbell? The balcony is pretty, with a palm tree on it. If I could, I would move in there immediately. You should do that. Then we can sit on the balcony and drink hot chocolate. Or swim in the pool."

"You don't even know if there is a pool."

"There is one. I have a feeling." I got goose bumps. Grandmother was simultaneously asking me questions that I answered with random nods or shakes of the head.

"He has a pretty wife. Long blond hair, like out of a commercial," said Vera.

"You're just making that up."

"He has two daughters."

"Stop," I said.

"Whatever you say," Vera answered, hanging up.

That night I didn't hear any footsteps. I woke up because I had to go to the bathroom. I walked past the two sleeping women into the bathroom until I felt a draft. The door to the staircase was open, much wider than the last time.

It didn't occur to me to wake up Grandmother or Nina. I slipped into my boots, barefoot, threw my jacket on over my pajamas, and ran out. First I went up the stairs because I couldn't shake the image of my grandfather on the roof. But the door that went to the roof was locked. I ran downstairs and out of the building.

It was cold, I slipped down on the wet sidewalk, got back up, and kept running. The playground looked spooky in the sickly light of the streetlamps. I searched park benches because I hoped he'd sat down somewhere to catch his breath. Every few minutes the headlights of a passing car shone on me. Despite the cold I was sweating beneath my jacket.

I felt as if I'd been looking for hours, but a glance at the time corrected me: not even thirty minutes. I decided to turn around, maybe he had long since gone back home. The beads of sweat on my forehead felt icy.

Back at the door to the building, I realized I had done everything wrong. I should have gone in the other direction. At first I took him for a shadow at the side of the road, until I got closer and leaned over him. Like me he was wearing a jacket over his pajamas, he had his eyes closed and was smiling.

THE MAN OF THE HOUSE

L eave your eyes closed, Father," said Grandmother. "I know that you hear me. Look, how you're lying there, like an angel, like Maya. You were always a good husband to me. Golden hands, we say. All your offspring have your slit eyes, even the little Jew, probably for seven generations. There's something of you still on this earth, Father. The boys have your thick Asian skin, you looked younger than me with every passing year, soon people would probably have taken me for your mother. Why did you do it? Why did you leave me like this? I've gotten through other things, but Nina there in the corner, she's weak. You've dumped all your baggage on me and then taken off. What does she have, anyway, that I don't have, those slim piano fingers or maybe the doe eyes? If somebody had treated me like a doe, then I would have had a look like that, but there was no deer where I was concerned. I was the exhausted racehorse, after that a beaten pack animal, but I won't let them make soap out of me. Stop crying, Nina, otherwise he won't be able to understand what I'm saying. And it is my request that he hear it.

"If there is one thing I regret, Father, then it's what I said about Maya. You didn't kill Maya. It was both of us. And you'll soon be with her. You've never since let down your loved ones again."

The floor slipped out from under my feet, and I only came to again when Grandmother bored into my upper arm with her pointer finger.

"Get up," she said.

I jumped up immediately.

"You're the man of the house now."

I had feared that Grandmother and Nina would be at each other's throats over the details of the funeral, but I was surprised.

"Nina, you are a musical person and have something like taste. I'm overwhelmed picking out the right coffin. My dead husband Tschingis Tschingisovich, peace upon his soul and may the earth be like down feathers to him, was a humble man and would certainly have chosen the simplest one for himself. On the other hand, I fear that might be construed by outsiders as a sign of disrespect or, god forbid, greed. I ask for your opinion."

"Just do what you want, Margarita Ivanovna. Like always. What outsiders are you talking about anyway? Are you expecting family?"

"A boil upon your tongue. Tschingis Tschingisovich's family is beyond me. They wanted nothing more to do with him after he'd decided upon me. Can you imagine that, his aunts called me old back then. I could have been his mother, they said."

"How impolite."

For the funeral, Nina lent Grandmother a black turtleneck, and for her part she was able to spare an unworn pair of black nylons. The funeral party consisted of the two of them, Vera, Tschingis, and me. Anastassia represented the rest of the world, and she looked breathtaking in her short black dress. Unfortunately I didn't have much of an opportunity to look at her because Vera kept trying to put her hand in my jacket pocket the whole time, supposedly because she was cold. She whispered something in my ear at the same time.

"Do you remember?" she asked, as if there was nothing more important in the world at that moment.

"Remember what?"

"When we were little and not here yet. We didn't know each other yet. All the snow in winter. Higher than I was tall. You walked along and didn't see anything but snow."

I nodded. "It was tough to walk. You were boxed in from head to foot."

"And those felt boots. As ugly as night."

"At least they didn't pinch."

"Mama always pulled me in a sled," said Vera.

Somewhere in her sentence a barely visible arrow was concealed. It stuck in me, and I had difficulty breathing.

"What is it?" she asked. "Didn't your grandmother pull you along on a sled? In the morning, to preschool?"

"I wasn't in preschool," I whispered back. "I was an idiot with no life expectancy."

"And did you ever lick a metal pole during the winter?"

"What pole?"

"Any. Swing set. Scaffolding."

I shook my head.

"Mama poured hot water over my tongue," said Vera, lost in thought.

I noticed belatedly that we were already standing at the side of an open grave and Grandmother was saying to a man in black: "You going to get on with it, or are you being paid by the minute?"

"Others wish to join." The man made a solemn gesture.

We all turned around simultaneously. The gate of the cemetery was open, and a mass of people streamed toward us. It was exclusively men, predominantly small ones, with dark faces, tanned skin, hair combed back. A few of them wore poorly fitting black suits, others wore overalls over which they'd thrown dark jackets or sweaters. They nodded to my grandmother from a distance, and with a precise delay of two seconds they repeated the gesture in Nina's direction. They lined up next to each other in several rows, and the little cemetery was suddenly full.

Nina cast a worried look at Grandmother. Grandmother squinted.

"Now let's finally get going, your honor," she said in Russian, and the funeral speaker closed his eyes and gave a brief speech, during which he pronounced my grandfather's name wrong.

With numb fingers we tossed a few clumps of moist dirt onto the coffin and stood to the side to let the men come forward.

They all watched silently as the grave was filled in. After that the men went past us. They stopped in front of me one by one and put out their hands. I shook all the hands extended to me. One pair of eyes after the next looked me in the face, and I had the feeling that it was my grandfather who wanted to tell me something that I didn't understand because I'd never learned the language of these men. I basically only now realized that it was even a language.

The men left without dignifying the women with so much as one more glance.

"Look!" said Grandmother full of amazement. "That's how you treat a widow. Asian mugs, I don't mean that as an insult, my dead husband was one himself, but they do have manners."

The cemetery emptied, we stood there just the six of us again. Anastassia looked furtively at her watch.

"Should we go to McDonald's?" asked Vera. Nina's enraged look, which was actually intended for her daughter, cut through me as well.

"Why not," said Grandmother. "Nastenka, dear child, I thank you for being part of this. You can go. Don't want the dance lessons to start too late. Your husband hasn't died. Oh my God, sweet Jesus Christ, I'm already talking like the dying Jew from that joke. Do you know it? *Is everyone here? Really, everyone? So who is manning the shop?* It's rubbing off on me."

Anastassia kissed each of us three times on the cheek, wiped her lipstick from the corner of my mouth, and made her exit.

Grandmother turned to me. "Speak of the devil. To the left of the gate."

She linked arms with Nina and headed toward the exit. Vera and Tschingis followed, I trailed after them. I saw him standing there, hands buried deep in his pockets. My grandmother strutted right past him without so much as a glance at him.

I stopped in front of him and also stuck my hands in my pockets, only to take them out again immediately. The last thing I needed was to start mimicking his gestures.

"What are you doing here?" I asked.

His lips moved, and his eyelid twitched. He said something, but the wind whooshed in my ears. My family continued on, and I was afraid I wouldn't be able to catch up to them because of him.

TRAITOR

Grandmother was worried about Nina.

"Still crying," was the first thing she reported to me when I came home from school. "I've got the little one on my lap night and day because she's incapable of doing anything. She's acting as if *her* husband died. I'm afraid she'll get depressed. First depression, then cancer, that's the way it always goes. And you? Able to understand something in school today?"

She paused for a second as if she really expected an answer, but then kept talking before I could open my mouth.

"All that crying won't bring him back, you know. I told her that, but it didn't help. Just cried more. I could tell her that he didn't really care much about her in the last few years. You could see that. But that wouldn't console her, do you think?"

This time the pause was long enough for an answer: "I don't think so."

"I mean, it's not as if I won't miss him. I look at those poor devils he works with . . . worked with, and I think: they're just like him and also somehow different. Their faces are expressionless, their gazes empty. Tschingis was a quiet man, but smart. He loved me so much, did everything for me, kneeled down in front of me just to get me to agree to marriage. I left the stage for him. Not because I was too old. Not because of the broken toes. Because of him. Everything for the family. Always the family that drags you down and breaks you. You know, I can't do everything—three children and a depressed woman and all the construction sites. Everyone has limits."

*

I'd taken Vera to the train station because none of the adults had thought of it. I'd asked her to stay, but she just snorted at the idea. "Where? In this hole? Without your grandfather it makes no sense."

I felt guilty because I couldn't offer her anything better, and because unlike her, I hadn't cried over Grandfather. When Vera called me uncaring and weird, I didn't contradict her. I could have said I just didn't have time to mourn because I could barely find a moment of peace. I'd seen how important it was for Grandmother to stay busy. Under Grandmother's watchful, unwavering gaze I did the cleaning, played with little Tschingis, even cut his toenails. Silence came only when she remembered I was a traitor, that I had embraced the enemy. Then she stopped talking to me for a while. I enjoyed it so much that I couldn't be sad during those moments, either.

Grandmother never maintained her silence for long, though. First she gave me angry looks. Later she mumbled into her knitting: "No wonder he sold out Grandmother. After all that I've done for him. He's caught up physically but inside everything is still a mess. No backbone, no character. What does the red-haired Jew have that allows him to buy you?"

I said nothing.

"Just refuse to talk, you. Of course he has a nice place. Given how many people's teeth he's pulled out. I've seen his business card. He didn't even keep his real name. He used to be named Maltchik and now all of a sudden he's Herr Doctor Mahl! Ridiculous. He sold his soul, so what should one expect from his spawn? You can work so much on a child, but it's all for nothing if the genes are bad."

"All we did was have cake together."

"What kind?"

"Chocolate mousse cake."

"I knew it. Raw eggs, salmonella. I'm sure your stomach hurt afterwards."

That wasn't the case, but I didn't correct her.

"Next time he'll put something in the cake, then you'll wake up at his place, in the basement, locked in with seven locks. Do you know the story of the father who kept his daughter locked up for fourteen years?"

I thought of my father's twitchy eyelid, the unbearable conscience-stricken look on his face. He was so happy when I'd finally called him. He'd shown me a photo of two girls at the café and said they were my sisters, two and four years older than me. They had strawberry blonde hair and were holding each other tight. They were gorgeous, and I had asked him if I could keep the picture. He gave it to me with obvious unease.

When I told Vera about the meeting, she asked: "Did you go out on the balcony? Is the palm tree real?" and was disappointed at my lack of progress.

"Just wait and see," grumbled Grandmother into a cooking pot where an indistinguishable substance was bubbling. "Tomorrow, no, maybe the day after he'll come again. He'll ask you all innocently: shall I buy you a puppy, Maxi? A real Great Dane? Do you want to come on vacation with me? Would you like a million? Dentists are rich because they always swindle people. Maybe you'll become one. When you were still little you were dependable. You were the best child in the world, a golden boy, my great hope. I gave you my life, and when you leave me, Maxi, I will no longer exist. I can endure a lot, but not that. Then I'll be on your conscience."

"Why would you say something like that?"

"Be quiet. I'm not speaking to you."

I was almost thankful to Nina for running Grandmother so ragged. Grandmother had to get her out of bed every day. "I know you're prone to depression, madam. But you can't do this to me. We have children." She took Nina tea in bed, sometimes also a moist washcloth: "Freshen up your face, my dear, then you'll feel human again and look a bit more human, too."

She would have made a corpse get out of bed. Nina gave in and staggered into the bath. When she came out, Grandmother was already waiting for her. "I've ironed this blouse for you, put it on, soon you won't have the figure for it anymore. We're not getting any younger. You can't hang about in your bathrobe all day, we're raising young men here, do you want Max to end up gay for good? That's better, brave girl. Where's your brush? Here, I cleaned it specially. Margo will do your hair nicely for you. And now a couple spoons of oatmeal, and then help Margo with the chores, I can't always slog away on my own."

She worked her way through Grandfather's belongings, washed the clothes, ironed them, and with Nina in tow gave everything away to the construction workers. Grandfather hadn't owned much, a few shirts and pants, a warm sweater, but his jacket and winter coat were, according to Grandmother, "of good quality. I bought inexpensive things, but never cheap things." She was pleased to find takers for all the clothing items, even the socks and underwear. Even years later, whenever I saw a man who reminded me of one of my grandfather's workers, I wondered whether he might be wearing one of his undershirts.

Once Grandmother had forgotten that I was a traitor, she consulted with me on questions concerning Nina's condition or our future.

"Why are you asking *me*?" I said every time. "Just give her a pill from the pill pouch, like you used to do for me."

"You are now the man of the house. Why do I have to decide everything on my own?"

"Grandfather never had to decide things, he always just did what you wanted."

"Is the red-haired Jew talking through you? What has he been telling you about us? Did you sit there eating cake, listening to your Oma get dragged through the mud?"

Grandmother no longer trusted me. When she didn't need my assistance with Nina, she wanted to know about every second of my life. When I came home late from school, she greeted me drowned in tears.

"I thought he'd snatched you again."

"Who would want me?"

"Now that you're no longer an idiot, maybe he does want you. Any moron would take such a fully formed boy. He should have seen you three years ago!"

"He tried the whole time. He wanted to support you guys. He sent me Christmas gifts that you hid from me. You just cursed his name. You told me about him only because I was allowed into Germany because of him, and you with me."

"Aha! I knew it! You met him again and he told you lies about your grandmother."

I'd seen my father three times since the funeral. He'd given me another business card, but I had long since committed his phone number and address to memory, and Vera had, too. Suddenly I had a father about whom I knew some key things: he no longer looked like he used to, and I could assign a place on the map and a telephone number to him. I repeated the number to myself every night before falling asleep. Sometimes I wrote it down and blotted it out immediately so Grandmother didn't get suspicious. When I lay in bed at night, I also repeated the things he'd said to me during our second meeting.

Your grandmother is a sick woman. She's mentally disturbed, she never recovered from the blow fate dealt her back then. One appearance in family court is all it would take and the rest would be child's play for me. But we don't want it to come to that. We want to try to settle it amicably. Your grandfather is dead, I always considered him the more sensible of the two. I don't want to think about what must be going on with you guys now.

I remembered the feeling, as if something had lodged in my throat, even though I hadn't touched the cake that he'd ordered for me. An invisible rope had constricted my ribs and tightened with every breath while I tried to explain my view of things to him. He was a stranger to me, I'd been afraid of him my entire childhood, and I couldn't get used to the fact that he was just a person. I met him and felt like a criminal every time because he thought only of me and not about my grand-mother's well-being. "She won't survive it. I'm the man of the house."

"You're still a child." He tried to put his hand on mine, I pulled it back. "You can call me anytime. You're always wel-come. Soon you'll be able to make up your own mind anyway about who you want to live with. Why are you shaking your head? You don't have to do this to yourself. You're still a child."

Nina continued to cry every day, and Grandmother felt guilty, as if she had killed Grandfather with her own hands. They went together to the cemetery, Nina kneeled down and cleaned the brass letters on the gravestone with a toothbrush while Grandmother braced herself by linking arms with me and then pointed with her free hand at spots Nina had missed.

"You have to give up this Eastern thing, Nina. We can't go around planting lilacs everywhere. The only people who do that are Russian women who've never seen roses. We need roses, Nina. Our Tschingis shouldn't remain the eternal slit-eyed Jew here, he should be one of them. How did you put it recently, Maxi? That absurd word? Integration. O.K., dry your eyes now, for all I care a lilac bush would be fine. You're lucky old Margo has a soft heart. The old man, just to get this on record, wouldn't have liked your flower ideas. Isn't that right, Maxi?"

I held Tschingis with my free hand and said nothing.

"You know what? I'll buy the woman some jewelry," Grandmother said later, when Nina had gone back to bed again. "A nice necklace. I always wanted jewelry. Once I had a suitor who gave me lots of it. I had to sell it all later so I could buy bread. But Tschingis Tschingisovich had no taste, so I was happy that he never gave me jewelry. But I was left without jewelry." She laughed, and her gold tooth blinded me. "I'll buy the depressed woman jewelry. She's certainly never gotten any before. She'll get the first piece ever in her life from Margo."

THE BRAID

I needed to sleep a lot during those days. I had crazy dreams: about a giant red-haired clown jiggling me while I was lying in a stroller, and about Grandmother wearing my grandfather's suit and getting married to Nina. I stood next to them and threw rice. My father was there, too, this time without the red clown wig, and he clapped his hands, which was difficult because his hands were trembling. A thought shot through my head: how can he drill teeth with hands like that? I heard a voice from above, thundering through the clouds: "YOU DIDN'T KILL MAYA. YOU JUST GOT THERE TOO LATE TO HELP HER. YOU HAD NO WAY OF KNOWING THAT SHE HAD A RUPTURED APPENDIX."

"It's called murder!" Grandmother screamed back.

"IT'S CALLED STUPIDITY AND STUBBORNNESS," thundered from the clouds.

"I thought it was the milk coming in!" yelled Grandmother, her face raised to the sky, her eyes closed so as not to be blinded by the light. "I told Tschingis Tschingisovich that a daughter who sleeps with a married Jew cannot expect any support, and he should relay that to her over the phone! He always did whatever I wanted! I had no way of knowing that she'd suddenly get so sick out of the blue, she never complained! But I was always alone in my damn life! And you don't even exist!"

One day when I was on my way home from school and nearly walked into traffic without noticing, Grandmother met me at the door. "You're too late. Were you at his place?"

"Whose place?"

"The Jew's place."

"Stop calling him that."

"You always have to pick a fight with Oma. Come here and help. The woman can't do anything again today."

She led me into the bathroom. Next to the tub was the chair she always sat on to dye her hair. The newspapers she usually spread out on the floor were missing, and besides, I'd just dyed her hair ten days before.

She sat down and handed me the large household scissors.

"What are you doing?"

"It has to go."

"Why?!" I felt panic rising, as if she were asking me to cut off her arm.

"Don't ask stupid questions. I can't work with it. Just gets in the way. There are men at the construction sites. There's no dancing at the construction sites."

"But why cut it off? Just put a scarf over it."

"Don't be an idiot. What kind of man would I be with a scarf on my head? Don't you want to help Oma?" She grabbed the braid with her left hand and started to hack at it with the scissors in her right hand. The stubborn hair wasn't easily cut, even when some individual strands escaped the braid.

"Don't!" I yelled.

"I'm going to build a house the way Tschingis Tschingisovich wanted to build it. White, clean, like the Germans. I already know where." She said the name of the most bourgeois development in the city. "Woods, a baker. No foreigners. Tschingis will have his own room and that fat ill-bred girl can have one, too, for all I care."

"And me?" My throat was dry. Grandmother had managed

to do it by this point. The braid fell into my hands like a dead animal.

"Put a rubber band around the loose end," she ordered. "Wrap it in newspaper. Take it with you as a remembrance. You're going to leave me soon. I can sense a traitor from kilometers away."

"Why would you say something like that?" I was nearly crying.

"The same thing will happen to you one day." She waved the scissors at me threateningly, pulled on the leftover fringe of henna-dyed hair, and shook her head disapprovingly. "You hang your heart on someone, do everything for him, sacrifice your life, and then he leaves you, newly widowed, with a depressed woman and two innocent children."

"What are you talking about?"

"You. You don't love Oma anymore. You're practically already gone."

"That's not true!"

"I can see it." She put her face close to mine so that I could see my own reflection in her pupils. "I see it," she repeated emphatically, and pushed me away.

And even though I was slow on the uptake, I understood what she wanted from me even before she said it: "Get out of here already!"

Obviously I didn't take the braid with me. I wrapped it in newspaper as instructed and put it in the drawer with my T-shirts. I was a little disgusted by it.

I took barely anything with me, not even a toothbrush.

You're always welcome, my father's voice echoed in my ears. *We have everything. Anything missing we will get.*

I went extra slowly even though I wanted to run. Down the stairs, to the tram that took me to the U-Bahn. I didn't run up the escalator, instead I stood still, then at the top I crossed the road. I'd looked at it on the map often enough. Even so, the trip to the white building was astonishingly short, the whole time it was so much closer than I'd ever imagined.

What would I do if he wasn't there? What would I say to his beautiful wife? His daughters? Would they send me away?

But he opened the door himself.

"I'm here," I said. His eyelid twitched.

The phone rang shortly before Christmas.

"Traitor," said Grandmother. "You never call."

"I have called and every time you've hung up."

"Uncle Jegor has died," said Grandmother.

"I'm sorry." I had no idea who she was talking about.

"I'm not. He was a liar and a miser. Wait. Stay on the line."

Something rattled and fell. Then came the sound of a piano. Grandmother played several wrong notes, and I heard her swear.

"What was that?" she asked when she finally finished.

"Waltz number two."

"You can recognize it, right?"

"Of course."

"You probably hoped otherwise but the old lady isn't dead yet. I'm going to live a long time yet, you hear? Longer than all of you put together."

"I believe you," I said, and it was the absolute truth.